QUICK KILLS

ALSO BY LYNN LURIE

Corner of the Dead 2008

QUICK KILLS

BY
LYNN LURIE

etruscan press

Etruscan Press
Wilkes University
84 West South Street
Wilkes-Barre, PA 18766
(570) 408-4546

www.etruscanpress.org

Published 2014 by Etruscan Press
Printed in the United States of America
Cover photograph by Margrit Polak
Cover design by Carey Schwartzburt
Interior design and typesetting by Susan Leonard
The text of this book is set in Garamond Premier Pro.

The excerpt on page 47 is from "Slash and Thrust" by John Sanchez reprinted with the permission of Paladin Press.

First Edition

14 15 16 17 18 5 4 3 2 1

Library of Congress Cataloging-in-Publication Data

Lurie, Lynn, 1958-
  Quick kills / by Lynn Lurie. -- First edition.
    pages cm
  ISBN 978-0-9886922-8-2 (alk. paper)
  1. Sisters--Fiction. 2. Family secrets--Fiction. 3. Women--Crimes against--Fiction. I. Title.
  PS3612.U774Q85 2014
  813'.6--dc23
                    2014009902

Please turn to the back of this book for a list of the sustaining funders of Etruscan Press.

For Franny

Doe, a deer, a female deer
Ray, a drop of golden sun
Me, a name I call myself

ACKNOWLEDGEMENTS

Many thanks to Terese Svoboda, wise and tireless reader, teacher and friend, to Noy Holland for a beginning and to Phil Brady for the continuation, and to those who most matter, Andrew, Barnett and Franny.

QUICK KILLS

◀ ◀ ◀

I am limp in his arms as he rushes me inside. So many stingers the nurses lose count. I hear the sound of their rubber-soled shoes as they move across the linoleum. I am unable to open my eyes. Maybe they closed them the way I have seen in the movies. I want no one to see me, not even when I am dead.

He takes me from the emergency room to my parent's house. I bend over for the spare key my parents keep under the WELCOME mat and feel how swollen my face is. The Photographer waits on the front stoop while I go inside.

Flickering candles on the dining room table turn the seated guests into shadows that rise and fall across the raised velvet wallpaper. Mother sees me first and gasps.

Hornets, I say slowly. Maybe wasps. My mouth is swollen shut on the left side.

Where were you?

The Photographer, he knew what to do.

Father does not look up from his conversation with the woman to his left.

I was going to tell them he is no savior but the maids were serving dessert.

I'm ok, really, I am. On my way to the stairs I stop at the front door and wave the Photographer on.

Mother and Father didn't even know I was out. I hear the Photographer's car turn the corner and the last sound I am able to make out before I fall asleep is Mother's high-pitched giggle, the one she uses when she isn't amused, then, I hear everyone's laughter.

For the next year an allergist threads tiny needles beneath the skin on my inner wrist, injecting dozens of allergens. I ask if this is necessary, after all I know what caused it—wasps or hornets—I saw the hive.

Eventually the doctor says I am desensitized.

I n the photographs he takes that afternoon, I am naked in an abandoned swimming pool. Rainwater has collected at the deep end and last year's dead leaves float across the surface. The trees aren't yet bare, their leaves having only begun to turn color. He has me stand ankle deep in the water before ordering me onto my back.

I make a face.

In the dry part then. He points to the far corner. Lie down and spread your hair above your head, like a halo.

Our first excursion was to the Bronx Zoo. The Photographer wanted to shoot me holding a python. The snakemaster wrapped the thickest, blackest one around my shoulders. An employee of the zoo offered to take a picture of the python and me with the Photographer, referring to me as the Photographer's daughter. At that moment the snake picked up its head and began to slither towards my face. I did not scream. I pleaded with the snakemaster to take the python off me.

After the snake was in its tank, I washed my hands with a special soap. One wash was not enough. He let me wash as many times as I wanted, until he said it was possible the soap could burn a hole in my skin.

There is fear in my eyes. I see the fear clearly even in the blurred snapshot. The adults waiting in line with their children must have seen it too. Fear like I have seen in my sister's eyes when she stood outside the kitchen door, craning her neck inside. Her back arched, she was prepared to turn away if Father was still seated in front of his orange juice and toast. When she saw that his spot was empty, that his juice glass had been drained, her eyes lost their intensity. It is the same fear the artist captured in the painting he made of my sister, myself, and my brother that hangs above the love seat in our parents' house, although he didn't put the fear into my sister's eyes, but into mine.

Years later when I visualize my death it is in the same woods where the swarm rose from the ground. My clothes are on and I am wearing my winter coat. Once settled into a tiny pit I have dug with my hands, I cover myself with fallen leaves and swallow the pills I have been stealing from my sister and Mother and hoarding ever since I first went to the Photographer's house.

◀ ◀ ◀

A mucus-like patch more brown than red and now I cannot keep my favorite pair of underpants. I carry them to school and stop in the alleyway behind the five-and-dime where I plan to toss them into the Dumpster. What if someone sees me or finds them and knows they belong to me? Then he or she will know what happened.

Instead, I will need to take a bus to a nearby town where I don't know anyone and find a quiet backstreet with a trash bin. When I'm sure I'm alone, I'll take the underpants, stuffed between American history and algebra, out of my school bag. When they are in the trash I will cover them with the garbage already there, the browned apple cores, the leftover spaghetti, and the wad of paper towels stained with rot and rain, and wait at the nearest corner to make sure no one has seen me.

After all the planning, I go to the Dumpster in the alleyway and fling the stained underpants over the side. They catch on the metal rim and hang there, the pattern of lilacs laced together with purple ribbons.

Mother calls upstairs. Dinnertime.

I already ate, I call back. Which could have been true, because the first time I went to the Photographer's house he made me dinner.

My pajamas are striped in red and white like the twine used to close a bakery box. Grandmother embroidered my name and Helen's on the shirt pockets to distinguish us. They insist on dressing us the same. I don't mind but Helen hates it and lets them know. Had Helen been home that night maybe I would have told her. I do not know if I would have said it was good or bad, or if I would have told her I had agreed.

I wake up gagging and run to the toilet, throwing up slippery water, and even when there is nothing left I do not feel better.

If Mother had asked to see the photographs the Photographer took I could not have shown her, not even one, as in almost every shot I am naked, and if I am clothed, I am either posed or making an expression that is inappropriate.

You said things to me, all sorts of things about my talent for photography. I now know it isn't a talent. But this was not your crime. You were nearly the same age as Father.

Young girls, you said, fill canvasses, and gave me a book of photographs of paintings by Renoir and Gauguin. I liked the one by Renoir where the girls, I imagined them to be sisters, maybe even twins in identical party dresses, are draped alongside a grand piano. They are awkward in their bodies and it shows in the way their shoulders are positioned. Still, they know how to be watched.

Helen preferred a photograph of a painting by Gauguin. A bare-breasted woman looks directly at the painter without shame, but without joy either.

You catalogue the pictures of me and file the negatives in a locked metal cabinet, occasionally offering me a print if there is one you are especially proud of. Anything you gave me is gone now, as are mostly all of the photographs I took then. I never took one of your face and I always had my camera with me.

◄ ◄ ◄

The Photographer and I shower in my parent's bathroom just one time. Afterwards, I don't know where to take him, so we go to dinner at the same restaurant we went to as a family on Sunday nights. Mother and Father would sit on the opposite side of the three of us. It always happened that Jake had to switch seats with Mother because he and Helen fought.

The Photographer is soon on his third bourbon.

I can't eat what I always order, a small steak served on white bread where the blood from the meat turns the bread a brownish red. It had always been my favorite part of the meal, the doused bloody bread.

When we return as a family I tell the waiter steamed mussels. Mother notices but doesn't ask why. I wish she had asked.

◄ ◄ ◄

The first funeral I went to was on a day of record cold. The son delivered the eulogy, and when he finished, the family took seats in a perfect line in the back of a limousine. The old lady wore black satin gloves that disappeared into her coat sleeves. A caravan of cars followed with their lights on. A thin veil of snow hit our windshield and made an icy sound that echoed. The ice stayed ice, it didn't melt or run.

No one took photographs even though he was painted back to life and his shirt collar was pressed. His cologne was so sweet it filled the funeral parlor and made my eyes tear. It seems now, because his frozen face is still so vivid, that I had been given a photograph of him as he lay there to take with me.

The coat Mother was wearing had once been alive. Silver fox, she said even though the fur was not silver and in picture books foxes were always red or brown. I rubbed my hand up and down her furry back until she pushed me away. I couldn't help myself and kept going back. There was nothing about the feel that made me think it was something that had died or that had been killed. Finally she said loudly, go away. Others must have heard because at that moment the machine lifting the casket paused and the creaking stopped. The casket, now lightly dusted in white, was suspended above a gaping hole.

When he was lowered into the ground, each mourner was expected to throw a shovelful of dirt across the coffin's shiny-varnished surface. My fingers were numb and Mother had forgotten my mittens. Still, she made me take the shovel, heavy with soil. The skin on the palm of my hand stuck to the handle the way my tongue stuck to cherry ice in summer. Helen turned away when I tried to give it to her. Rather than make a fuss, Mother took the shovel and passed it to the old man next to her. For that one time I wanted to be Helen.

The story we heard the rest of that winter and into the spring was how Patty Hearst had been kidnapped and sealed inside a coffin buried in the ground, even though she was still alive. The dead man looked so alive I was sure he, too, was breathing, that a mistake had been made. Even the newscaster couldn't say if Patty Hearst was kidnapped or if she had gone willingly, and he didn't answer the question everyone was asking, was she dead or was she alive?

Mother didn't cry at the funeral, and when I asked why, she said there wasn't anything that could have been done.

◀ ◀ ◀

Father was a hunter. He turned into our driveway after having been away all weekend. Strapped to the roof of his gold-colored Buick were two dead deer. A trail of blood had hardened on the back windshield. I stared at the carcasses because at first I didn't know what they were. At the same time Helen realized it, so did I. She screamed so loudly Mother rushed outside wearing her apron with the pine trees, her hands covered in ground meat. Daddy, Helen cried in the direction of the house, killed Bambi and her little sister.

He didn't mount the heads or preserve the skins but he did gut them on our drive, the same drive where we rode our bicycles and played hopscotch after drawing the outline of the board with chalk. And even though he washed the pavement when he was finished, I was sure little pieces of bone or skin had caught in the rutted surfaces or settled in a shallow corner. I avoided all the corners, sure there was something remaining, a tuft of fur, a tooth. He scrubbed the car windows clean, the metal door handles, too.

Mother froze the deer meat in plastic but never made us eat it. She didn't touch it either, except to fry it in the pan. Father was the only one.

◀ ◀ ◀

Father wants to capture us as children and hang us on the wall above the love seat in the living room. To do this Mother takes us to the artist's house to the part out back he calls his studio. We have to sit an hour a week and each of us goes on a different day because we can't patiently wait our turn and then be poised and obedient.

Monday is my day. Monday mornings Mother worries about the creases in my jumper. I come to breakfast dressed but still she makes me remove the jumper and has me stand in my socks, shoes, and underwear at the ironing board while the maid runs the iron up and down the front of my dress. There are three pleats that begin at the collar and come to an end at the hemline, which is stitched in a zigzag of red. Father sips his coffee and watches me, not even pretending to read the morning paper. When Mother says the pleats are perfect, I put the dress on without waiting for it to cool. I would rather burn my skin than stand in front of Father for even one more second half-dressed.

Mother reminds me to hurry outside to the car as soon as the last bell rings. But I make her wait, having told my teacher Monday is a good day for me to wash the blackboards, which is why I am never the first one out and why, when I do appear, I am covered in chalk dust.

Mother doesn't like the drive, especially in winter when it gets dark early. The unpaved road cuts through the woods where men come to shoot deer. I open the car window and listen for the sound of shots even though I have never heard any. Mother gets cold easily and insists I close the window. With my forehead pressed against the glass, I look for bloodstained patches of ground but I have never seen any.

The artist tells me to fold my hands and when he isn't satisfied he comes over and bends down on one knee. Using both of his hands he moves mine, touching my fingers, placing them like tiny sculptures across my pink lap. It is each finger he wants to see. I don't like him watching me so closely. Even so, I ask Mother if she has a ring I can wear. I imagine a pink stone in the shape of a diamond, but she doesn't have a ring or any other jewelry, not for me.

Now when I think of my brother and sister as children, the faces I see are the ones the artist painted. Helen's hair is parted slightly off-center. He captured the dazed look she already had in her eyes at the age of thirteen. Seated below her is my brother holding the double-decker bus Father bought him in London. His lips are in a half-smile that looks more like a grimace.

When we are not with the artist, he works off black-and-white photographs taped to the wooden frame of his easel. He told Mother he needs to see me even when I am not there in order to draw me more perfectly. Sometimes he changes the placement of the photographs, but never eliminates any. He asks Mother about my habit of biting my nails. Of Helen he wants to know about the bruises, and as to my brother, why all the politeness?

In one photograph Father's arm is around my waist. I remember trying to inch away and him pulling me back. The artist says I look like Father, more so than Helen or Jake. He insists my legs be crossed with each shoe facing forward, my socks folded in a straight line even though no little girl would sit this way. If the scene isn't how he wants it, he leaves the brush on the easel's wooden ledge and comes in so close I can hear his heart beating. His hands stink of turpentine. When he touches my chin or tucks a loose hair behind my ear the odor makes me drowsy. I must stay awake watching him, making sure he doesn't come in closer and touch me again. Later, at home in front of my mirror, I practice staying focused. There are nights I am in bed and feel my skin burning. It is the artist looking at me.

He does not paint our marks, our bruises or scrapes, not even a rumpled skirt. There is a framed photograph on the wall across from where he works. I can't say what it is because the head is missing; it is some sort of water animal, maybe a hippopotamus or rhinoceros. In houses of my friends and in a club my Father takes us to, I have seen halls lined in hanging heads. In his photograph, perfectly perched on top of the rotting animal is a very white bird. It is different from the wooded scenes hanging in my parents' paneled den—deer at streams or roosters outside a barn where everything is drawn to scale. It seems beautiful because of the light, but there is a trick to looking at it, to seeing what it is exactly.

I never know how much time is left until I hear Mother's car pull into his gravel driveway. And I never ask. Here in the South, we have been told children should not speak unless spoken to. When Mother picks me up, I am so tired from being still and from worrying about the artist and what he is doing that I sleep the entire drive home, waking with the print of the seatbelt patterned into my cheek. Saliva is crusted on the outside corner of my mouth and my left arm is pins and needles. It is an awful thing this sleep, and every Monday night, no matter how late I go to bed, I lie wide-awake watching the hands on the clock.

The three of us are standing in my parents' house, not the one where we grew up but the one they moved to at the end of their lives. It's a ranch because Father can no longer walk up stairs. The box-like home sits on a flat piece of property overlooking the woods. Father spends his afternoons on the back deck bundled beneath a blanket. Seated on a plastic-latticed lawn chair, he stares into the trees hoping to see a family of deer grazing on the lawn or leaping over the wire fence that divides his property from the neighbor's.

The oil painting of us as children now leans against the wall with all their other paintings, the old man with the captain's wheel in hand, the peeled orange on a dark mahogany credenza, a batik from Thailand of two dancers and a trio of flowers at different intervals of budding. My brother turns the picture of us around so the image faces the wall. Helen doesn't want it either. None of us, she says, ever looked that way.

Remember having to sit for him? I ask. How impatient he was and how long it took, that way he stared at you, as if he knew everything about you.

I don't remember, Helen says.

◀ ◀ ◀

Even in photographs, Mother's hairpiece doesn't look real. She keeps it bobby-pinned to a Styrofoam head that sits on her vanity. In the late afternoon, anticipating a dinner party, she brushes each shaft the way the sales lady instructed, then, positions it on her head using the combs sewn inside the wig to attach it to her scalp. Unlike Mother, the fall has straight long hair in many shades of brown. She wears a velvet headband to disguise the stitching of the wig.

Father likes the guests to hear how well Helen plays the piano. Before the performance the maid helps Helen with her hair, sweeping it from her face and piling it on top of her head. She plays Mother's childhood piano that Mother never plays. Before beginning, Helen stares at Mother hoping to get her attention. Mother casually leans against the wall and smokes her extra long cigarettes. She doesn't look at Helen but stares into the distance. For most of the night Mother is quiet. It is unusual to hear her speak except when she is telling the maid to do something.

Father's expression during the performance is of pleasure, and when Helen is done, she takes a bow and makes a curtsy. Some guests ask her questions. Others compliment her. It is true she is pretty when she smiles.

That night there is a commotion in Helen's room. I think Father must have disturbed her when he left a gift on her nightstand, which he does after she performs.

In the morning I ask Mother if Helen is okay.

A mouse scampered across her dresser and frightened her. Still, she insists on keeping food in her room.

But, I argue, Helen likes the mouse. She keeps the lifesavers in the dish next to her brush and comb so he will come. She even tries to wait up for him.

The gift Father gave Helen is a blue-eyed, blonde-haired Barbie. When I come home from school I find it on the floor alongside Helen's dirty clothing, undressed. Barbie's hair is in tangles. A pin from Helen's Girl Scout sash, the one she received for International Friendship, is in Barbie's eye. The gash is larger than the circle of blue.

There are other disturbances, and I wonder if our house is haunted like my friend Thea's, who lives on the plantation her family has owned for over a century, where slaves once grew tobacco. Their main house is lit by gas, which throws an eerie and unreliable light. Beneath the foundation are underground tunnels connected to storehouses. Her brother takes us through using a flashlight. Without warning he turns it off and rushes ahead. Thea pleads with him to come back, and when he doesn't, she starts to sob.

Get on your knees, I tell her, and use your hands to feel the wall on the left and the ground in front of you. Just crawl.

I can't without seeing. Do you know what's in this ground? All sorts of dead things. It is awful to even think about it.

Yuck. But you don't want to stay here. And besides we don't know if he is coming back.

When she doesn't move, I squeeze in front of her. The damp soil scrapes my knuckles. It still hurts, especially now as soil collects under the nail and then a shard of glass, or something sharp, cuts into my palm. I was in the tub when Father came in. I grabbed the shower curtain to wrap around me to hide myself, but he was pulling from the other end and my fingernail got caught in the crease. He kept pulling until the nail tore from its bed.

It's a joke. Her brother says and then turns on the flashlight.

Thea is huddled against the wall, her cheeks streaked with tears and soot. Above her head, iron hooks jut from the wall and the ground beneath is stained.

Animal blood, he says pointing, cows and chickens, what they ate back then, duck too, just like now.

The ground slopes as if the blood carved a shallow stream and its banks are tinted red. I see cow heads hung upside down so the blood can drain, then I see people, whole bodies, naked black men, the skin of their throats wrapped over the hand-hewn hooks, the way a jacket's hood loops over a metal store-bought hook.

Thea's mother and father sit at opposite ends of a very long table. We answer only when we are spoken to and we always begin with Sir or Ma'am and end with Thank You. The servants hover at the swinging door that leads into the kitchen. Our backs are to them, but when they approach to clear the table, the light of the chandelier outlines their dark faces, accentuating their white crisp shirts and ironed skirts, but even still I cannot see their expressions. The most they do is nod.

It is implied that not a bite of food is to be left. I wouldn't know for sure, but I think we are eating goose or maybe duck. Something I have never eaten, more the texture of chicken than steak, although the meat is grey and oily. Her parents do not look across the table or at each other. Their eyes are focused on their plates. At the end of the meal there isn't even dessert.

Tucked into Thea's bed, we stare at the frilly lace and ribbon canopy. Thea takes my hand. It's about Tilly, she whispers, the slave that haunts our house. She comes at night and stands at the side of the bed that you're on and waits for me to wake up. She stopped growing the day she gave birth to a daughter here in this room. She was thirteen and hadn't looked pregnant. When her baby came out more white than black, the midwife knew if she didn't kill it Tilly would have been sold as a field hand and sent away. She told her to rest, that she would wash and swaddle the baby, but instead she drowned her. When Tilly found out, she ran from the house wandering the fields, not remembering her name or who owned her. Now she comes back because she is still looking for where the baby is buried. I have been trying to help her but I can't find anything. In here, she pulls a composition book out from under a stack of comics, I keep a map of the places I've searched.

How can you tell?

By temperature. If the soil isn't warm it means the bones can't be there. Once you practice, I will show you tomorrow, you get the feel of it.

I hear Helen other nights. Like Tilly, she doesn't rest.

Usually I am able to get back to sleep, but on one night Mother and Father are speaking loudly. Father tells Mother to shut up, which is something we have been forbidden to say, especially now that we live in the South where manners and rules are important.

In the morning Mother isn't in their bedroom, and the heavy blanket from her side of the bed is strewn across the length of the couch. Father has already left, which explains why Mother doesn't wake Helen. He is the one who insists we don't miss a day of school even when we are sick. Mother hasn't put our juice and toast on the table.

I call to Mother. What happened last night? Why was everyone awake?

You must have dreamed it.

She doesn't say goodbye to Jake or to me, and she doesn't remind us to take our lunches.

Why does Helen get the day off?

Hurry, Mother says, I hear the bus.

◄ ◄ ◄

Father's father—the one Helen and I refer to as the rich one because he has a personal maid who dresses him in silk, manicures his nails, and sprays him evenly at morning and at night across his neck with French perfume—takes the family photographs.

We are standing on his balcony, overlooking the ocean in Miami Beach. Mother is off to the side wearing her fall and headband, brown pumps, pleated skirt, a pink lace blouse and pillbox hat. Father's arm is around Helen. He tries to draw her close but I can see her feet are resisting, like a tree in a strong wind, the way it must bend in order to survive. No one has noticed me, or if they have, they don't mind that I am wearing a tee shirt and a pair of crumpled pink and white shorts.

Click.

Father's father doesn't know about composition. His job is to make us look our best. The column looks as if it is growing out of Mother's head.

Say Cheese.

Click.

Then to Jake, stay still.

Click.

And to me, hold the dog or she can't be in the photographs.

Click.

Something, maybe the light of the flash or the noise, frightens Coco and she runs.

In the room adjacent to the terrace is a life-size painting of Father's father seated in a leather chair, even though he does not own a leather chair, and on his finger is a ring with a blue stone, which I have also never seen. In life he doesn't wear jewelry, not even a wedding band. But the artist drew his lips the way they are—thin and long. The nose, too, is accurate and to scale. His oily skin glistens. It is the sort of painting that might hang in a castle or government building, a portrait of a king or president.

Mother's father and mother live directly across the street with a view of a multi-level parking garage. Because we are the only grandchildren, we are required to spend half our vacation on one side of the street before switching to the other. Each one keeps track of the time, but Mother's mother, Mama, which she insists we call her because Grandmother dates her, makes the most trouble.

I go where they tell me but I am not the one they fight over. Jake's presence is worth more than my sister's or mine. I prefer to go across the street with Mother, my brother and sister, but a cousin of my Father, whom I have never met, is in Miami. The cousin's girlfriend has a son who is also thirteen. Father tells me I will be spending the day with them at Sea World.

It is always tense, the leaving of one grandparent's apartment for the other, and my parents begin to argue. I hope Mother is taking my side because today I'm supposed to be with her parents, not at Sea World.

I open the bedroom door and call out: Please don't make me go. Then I stand with my back against the closed door. Even with my fingers in my ears I have no luck blocking them out. Father tells Mother when I return from Sea World he will bring me across the street, or if it is too late, first thing in the morning.

The front door slams. Mother leaves.

I stare out the living room window onto Collins Avenue and count the cars going in the direction of the city. Mother stands on the median with my sister and brother and her American Tourister suitcase, color red. Had I run after them, she would have sent me back.

Father calls to me from the kitchen. I don't make him wait. On the table is a stack of recent photographs from his parents' anniversary. Because Father wanted pictures of both his parents, he took these. One is cut in half. Father sees me looking at it.

Your Mother, he says, should make sure she never looks this way again.

In the half he is discarding, Mother's eyes look like doll's eyes and the front of her dress is stained with red wine.

I want to know how long I have to be at Sea World but hesitate to ask, not wanting to remind him.

They will be picking you up in less than an hour, he says, go get pretty. He crumples the half of the picture that is Mother and throws it in the garbage.

My cousin keeps kissing his girlfriend's lips and biting her ear while his hand holds her ass that is wrapped in a tight red skirt. We sit on wooden bleachers and watch a show of dolphins. The sun is in my eyes. When the camera pans the crowd I cover my face. I do not want anyone to see me here, for there to be a record.

The ride home takes a very long time and the motion of the car, especially the starting and stopping, makes me feel sick. When they drop me at Father's parents', I am not feeling well and in the course of the night I develop a fever. By morning, Grandmother, who never speaks until after Grandfather has spoken, determines I have the flu.

Mother, my sister and brother must know I am sick, otherwise Father would have brought me across Collins Avenue according to plan. But Mother hasn't called to ask if I need medicine or to see a doctor.

Father's mother gives me a box of pink, scented tissues. Your father will get you lunch, she says. And here is mentholated chest rub in case your cough gets worse. Grandfather and I will be back in a few hours. You need to keep the window closed.

But it's so hot. I protest.

And I am going to keep the curtains drawn. Maybe you can sleep.

The television in the bedroom glows from its faux wood console. It is the winter of one of the Apollo missions and the news is on every channel. I keep seeing the same craters while I hear the deep voice of the newscaster, who isn't saying anything of interest. Father is also watching, but in the other room. Later, when he and Jake are together, they will talk about what they have seen, especially the spacecraft, the men in the blow-up suits and how everything, including the men, floats and drifts without reason.

I get out of bed and go into the bathroom where I spend a long time kneeling on the tile floor in front of the toilet, not sure if I am going to be sick. When I feel better, I get up to use the toilet. I am sitting on the plastic puffy seat leafing through Mother's *Cosmopolitan* magazine. My pajama bottoms are gathered at my ankles. The door opens. At first I think it is a mistake, that Father doesn't see me.

I close the magazine. It drops to the floor and makes a noise as it hits the tile. The cover is the typical *Cosmopolitan* photograph of a beautiful woman looking directly into the camera. I stare at her so I do not have to look at Father. She is wearing a gold lamé dress and her hair is in ringlets.

I remember Father saying, what's wrong with you? You don't know to close the door?

But the door was closed.

◀ ◀ ◀

Many years later Mother told me she went to a divorce lawyer when she was pregnant with Helen. The lawyer persuaded her to stay with Father, that if she were to leave she would end up destitute, unable to provide for Helen, whereas Father had economic promise.

Helen wasn't very old, and it was already clear to Mother that Father loved Helen more than anyone else in his world.

Helen calls from the water. Stop being scared. Think of all you're missing. I'll even hold your hand.

No. I call back. I am afraid of the tide. The waves are too high. Why even do you like it here?

The sound of the ocean, the taste of salt. She licks her inner wrist. The way I can get lost here.

Mama lies all day on her towel. Maybe she thinks the sun will turn her young. But the sand chafes my skin, scrapes my eyes, and gets caught in my belly button. They don't like it when I complain, so I walk away. If I keep moving the sand won't have time to stick.

The beach is the loneliest place, all one color and one sound. The echo of the waves is continuous, and even when I bring a shell to my ear, the kind that is pink and shiny inside, I cannot escape. All of it makes me sleepy, but I am afraid to sleep in the open where people can see me. Instead, I sit down and dig and don't stop until black tar sticks to my fingers. I'm going to claw my way to China. Mother once told me it is possible.

The song about popcorn and Crackerjacks is playing at the concession stand. I know the words. Mama tells me to smile but I don't know how to just do this, so I pretend she has a camera and is taking my picture. I want to be home counting the four walls and the cracks in the paint with the door to my room locked and the window shades pulled down.

As we are leaving, Helen begs Mama to buy her a beach ball. Mama keeps walking. Helen stomps her foot. You never buy us anything. Father's parents buy us whatever we want.

Mother's father asks the vendor. How much?

Mama turns and scowls at him.

Think how lovely she would look. He says, a photograph of Helen and the ball.

I can see Father wanting a picture of Helen in her bikini sitting on the ball with her legs spread wide, for balance.

◀ ◀ ◀

Father buys his guns in Florida. Helen sits next to him on the edge of the guest bed as he explains how the newest one is assembled. He allows her to look through the scope. She says he is in focus. I have never seen her hold onto anything so tightly. She is, just then, someone older and more determined than Helen ever was. And when she volunteers her suitcase to bring the gun home, Father disassembles it, places it in its velvet-lined case, before wedging it alongside Helen's cosmetics, her underwear, and brightly embroidered peasant blouses.

◀ ◀ ◀

Jake pushes Father's desk chair under the wooden rack. Above him, nearly reaching to the ceiling, are Father's hunting rifles.

Don't touch those. I tell him. He is going to know.

Jake takes down the one with the long barrel and looks through the scope as he points it at my head.

Don't do that, Father told us never do that.

It isn't loaded.

What if it is? What if he forgot?

Jake puts the rifle back.

It's lopsided. He's going to know.

Where do you think he keeps the key to the case with the pistols?

The skeleton key?

Yeah.

It's on his key chain that's always with him and that is exactly why, so you don't touch his guns.

Jake peers into the case. Some old lady sold them to Father. Do you think she knew how to use them?

If you don't get out of here, I am going to get Mother.

This bow is the coolest. He lifts it from the shelf. The mechanism is state of the art. It can totally destroy the target. Pow. Pow. Imagine it exploding into a million pieces.

I'm getting Mother.

Jake walks to the door. But stops at the closet to touch each one of Father's vests. There are boots and gloves and stacks of magazines that come each month with pictures of the newest gear and guns.

◄ ◄ ◄

Mother's father knows about composition, but when he draws trees he doesn't give them leaves, only needles. He wants only the leaves from his childhood that he saw from his bedroom window overlooking the port of Odessa. The trunk and the bark, even the branches come to him, but he is unable to remember the shape or size of the leaves.

I go with him to the library where he asks for books on trees, then on Russian painters from the turn of the century. He still can't remember. When his sister isn't able to help, he begins to sketch her. She is wedged elbow to elbow in the steerage compartment of the ship that brought them to America. He draws the hook and eye of her boots perfectly.

How do you remember that?

I laced and unlaced her boots to keep busy. She kept tally of how many times by scraping a notch in the wooden floor with a nail. At the end of the trip there were so many marks, one on top of the other, we couldn't count them.

Make me a picture of all the marks.

He draws hundreds of gouges in different lengths and widths, and the shape of all the marks together looks like a house.

Really, that's how it looked? So at the end of the trip she would have a house?

No, it just looks that way now but it wasn't in the shape of anything.

What color was your sister's scarf?

It was a traditional *babushka*.

Is that a Russian or a Yiddish word?

Both.

Which means he doesn't know.

The old lady on the boat next to us talked to herself and by the third day she was screaming. A man tied a *babushka* around her mouth and used a second one to pin her arms behind her. My mother told us not to worry, she said the old woman had gone mad. My sister wanted to know what that meant, to go mad.

Papa gives me his sketch. Mostly empty ovals and a knot of arms and legs, so many it is difficult to see which arms belong to which head. On every foot is a boot, the hooks and eyes drawn perfectly. The oval that is his sister is the only one with a face and an expression. Her left arm covers the right side of her face to shield her from what is coming towards her.

Mother's father wakes most nights after we have gone to sleep, calling out in Russian and in Yiddish. The infection in the bones of his legs that tormented him as a child is back. I pray for him each night before I go to sleep even though I have never done this before. When he begs Mother to kill him to end his pain, I am sure this is what it means to go mad. I escape his screaming by crawling between the mattress and the box spring.

One afternoon I come home from school and Papa and all his clothes are gone. We do not visit him in the hospital. Mother says children are not allowed, and when I ask if I can call him on the phone, she says it isn't possible.

Jake laughs. Maybe the mud reminds him of a cartoon he has seen. Roadrunner will fall from the cliff scorched by gunpowder and reappear as if nothing at all happened. No one else laughs. The caskets keep coming, emptying from the helicopter's hull. We watch silently until Jake interrupts, asking the names of the planes, badgering Father to explain how they are able to land in the jungle without a runway.

Mother's father is gone all winter and well into spring. After school Helen sits at the kitchen table and looks out the glass doors to our backyard that borders the neighbors. She says, I am teaching myself to draw snow using a white crayon from Papa's box of colors. The hardest part is the ice because it is between a liquid and a solid, on the edge of change and there are no twins.

Her flakes are not ordinary, not like the cutouts we made in first grade, more like the lace of a dress. When she's done, she covers it with a piece of tissue paper to protect it from smudging and asks Mother to bring it to Papa in the hospital. Father lifts the tissue to look at the picture. He tells Helen she is talented. I want to be that too, but Helen refuses to show me what she knows. When she isn't at the table, I try to trace her snowflakes using my finger, the way they curl and dead-end and start up again, one merging into the other. But when I take the crayon and try to reproduce what I just traced, my snow looks nothing like hers.

I begin sleepwalking. They tell me I resist being taken back to bed, repeating in a monotone, I am going to the hospital to visit Papa. When I wake in the morning I am not in my pajamas but fully dressed, my blouse and skirt crumpled. Worse though, I have no memory of what happened and I am afraid I might be going mad.

At the entrance to the school cafeteria is a table with individual cartons of milk and a dish for money. It's an honors system, three cents. I steal mine, pretending to pay. Some days I take back two pennies as if I left a nickel. The women in blue hairnets sell blue and pink iced cupcakes from behind the counter and each week I save the change that isn't mine until I have ten cents for one. After I finish eating, I squish the brown lunch bag into a ball and toss it into the garbage. But I see in the creases Papa's face and I am unable to leave it, even though it is covered in the mustard from the sandwich below and the milk I tossed in after.

I begin to store the creased bags and leftover food in my locker. Many times a day I ask to go to the bathroom or to the nurse's office so I can make sure that all the many Papas in my locker are okay. I count the bags, keeping track.

◄ ◄ ◄

In eighth grade Julie Farber walks across the country living off
people's garbage and sleeping in parked cars until a man finds
her outside his house in Los Angeles and brings her inside. Helen
knows the story from Julie's sister. All my classmates and I know
is that she isn't at her desk, or in homeroom, or anywhere else we
would look for her.

She's living with a man who takes care of her. Helen says.

Does she go to school?

Sort of. He is teaching her to be his lover.

He lives alone?

Apparently, and buys her silky black tops and other kinds
of clothes. When he's at work, a woman comes to the house and
waxes all the hair off her body.

Why?

It's sexy.

Do you think she's telling the truth?

Why wouldn't she?

Eventually Julie's parents bring her back. Three boys in our
grade, hoping to get a glance of her, spy on her house, waiting in
the bushes, sometimes working in shifts, but they have nothing to
report. There have been no sightings.

After a month she returns to her desk and is seated alongside
us in homeroom. She no longer takes the bus. Instead her mother
drives her in a car with the windows tinted black. Julie dresses the
way the rest of us do, in short skirts and tight-fitting shirts, but
when we ask for details she is vague. Instead she shows us her
manicure, and we study it as she touches the gold chain around her
neck. The sensation of the metal against her skin has the effect of
transporting her, maybe back to his house or in his arms. Her eyes
glaze over and her lips curl upwards in a half smile.

It was a gift. My birthstone is topaz. My parents don't know any of this. I plan to go back. His bed faces flowering bougainvillea trees.

She says bougainvillea with an accent but isn't concerned we might laugh at her, and none of us do, we wouldn't think of it, we are mesmerized.

I watch from across the room as she takes out her pencil and spiral notebook and study the way she uses the red eraser on a wheel. There is a style to her walk, as if she has been practicing.

The next girl to go is Andrea O'Brien. Andrea sits behind me in biology class and we have been cheating off each other all year. The question on the midterm that gets us into trouble is, "Why does the scrotum hang?" She writes and I copy, "For protection." The correct answer has something to do with the sperm needing to be cooler than the temperature of the body. The teacher brings us into the hallway and threatens to call our parents. Andrea doesn't care. Later that week she is gone. We hear she is a stowaway on a ship to the Panama Canal, but unlike Julie we are not able to verify this because she never returns.

For Helen, it is a girl from camp. Helen waits under the clock at Grand Central, and after counting three more trains from Rockville Centre, she calls Ronnie's house. Ronnie's parents know nothing more than they saw her get on the train that Helen met. Helen tries a few more times over the next year but the answer is always the same, Ronnie is gone.

◀ ◀ ◀

Mother must forget about me when I am with the Photographer. She doesn't know his last name, only where he lives, and not because she asked but because she drove me there one time. This was before I was old enough to drive. If only she had waited and seen how I hesitated at his door, the way I shuffled my feet as I looked through the dirty pane of glass. When I turned back all I saw through the leaves of the bushes that skirted his property was the red of her sports car as she entered the highway and sped away.

Another time I didn't stay. Instead I walked across the highway to a diner where the waitress was hardly old enough to work. I didn't have change for the jukebox at my booth, only enough for one coffee. The pay phone was at the back of the diner outside the bathroom, but Mother's phone just rang and rang.

I walked back to his house. He opened the door and held out his hands. They were shaking.

You can't stay. He stammered. Not today and I can't drive you home.

He stank of bourbon and when he reached for a chair to sit, he almost missed the seat.

I don't have money for the train.

I'll call a taxi. He said, then pointed upstairs.

Upstairs was a mess. Beside his wallet was a stack of photographs. I looked through them. The girl faced the camera. He had superimposed shadows across her face. Her body was just beginning to turn away from childhood, yet her expression belonged to an older woman. I viewed them as a series, like Edward Muybridge's males in motion where the penises flopped around.

The cab was honking its horn. I ordered the stack and pushed it closer to his wallet. One photograph fell. It was the only one I took with me. If the cab wasn't late and I did not have a train to catch, I would have gone back and taken them all. I should have gone back.

◀ ◀ ◀

The Photographer is at the front door waiting for me. Mother is talking about the sixth sense of dogs. He agrees with her that it is entirely possible, actually likely, when Father would have told her she was crazy, or worse yet, empty-headed. He tells Mother about a run-in he had with Con Edison, something about lunch and garbage. She is laughing and it isn't her fake laugh. I hear her invite him to Yom Kippur.

Dinner is the usual: round challah speckled with raisins, chicken and soup. The Photographer tries the Con Ed story on Father but he doesn't laugh. At temple I sit between him and Mother. Children run up the center row of the synagogue, collecting pledges for the war effort in Israel. The Photographer doesn't drop anything into the basket but Father does, as does everyone else in our pew. When the prayers start again, it sounds as if the choir is singing to the tune of *A Bicycle Built for Two*. Helen and I can't stop laughing. Every time I try to think of something sad to make me stop, Father dying, Mother leaving, I only laugh louder.

Mother tells us to get out of the sanctuary. Helen and I are doubled over and have trouble leaving our row without drawing even more attention to ourselves. I think Helen trips on someone's foot or maybe her own, which makes us laugh harder and louder. Mother is furious.

Later the Photographer tells me we acted like children. Mother punishes us. But it is him I hate.

◀ ◀ ◀

The Photographer has moved the headless mannequin to a far corner. **XXX** is scrawled across her middle. I know this because the mannequin and I share clothing.

As he slips her crinoline and tulle over the metal hook he tells me to get undressed. When I am standing in my underwear he throws me the crinoline to put on.

His video camera is mounted on the tripod and faces his bed dead center. The crumpled linen and headboard are in focus. His clothes are off. The video is set to record. The angle of my neck and the way the light falls on his face distorts his torso.

He places his knee on my chest to pin me down. Then points. That thing is parallel with the floor.

I look away.

When he needs to he gets up and reloads.

At home I put Helen's ballet tutu over my head to cover my face and creep into Jake's room. I hide in his closet while he is still in the bath. When it feels right, after Mother has tucked him in and gone downstairs, I enter Jake's room. I tell him I am the genie. He tells me what he wishes for. I want to shoot a gun perfectly straight. To never miss the target. And for Father to be there and to see it all.

We do this all winter. I even take the tutu to Florida until one night Helen comes into the room and turns on the light and pulls the crinoline away from my face. She holds the pink tutu above my head and makes it dance. I try to grab it back but she is too tall and too fast.

Our game is over.

When the Photographer is finished with his video, he goes downstairs to make himself a drink. He rattles around in the windowless kitchen with the grease-stained walls, returning with a cup of tea and a plate of toast for me. The toast is cut in perfect diagonals and spread evenly with red jam.

He turns on the television. I ask if I can watch *The Wizard of Oz*. Mother told me it was on. He wants to watch the Nixon impeachment hearing but lets me choose. My favorite part is when Dorothy pulls back the curtain and sees the wizard is a fraud.

The Photographer walks me to my parents' front door and apologizes to Father for getting me home late. He says *The Wizard of Oz* kept us.

◀ ◀ ◀

He crosses a field.
I trail behind.

He points to a gnarled tree. Spread across the thickest branch. Good, now press your stomach into the bark. The clothes are wrong, they need to come off, just drop them.

I do this.

The bark is rough, it scratches my stomach, and the weight of me draws last night's dampness from the branches, causing goose bumps to rise on my arms. I am staring at my fingers wrapped tightly around the branch holding me in place.

I try to distort his voice so the words don't come to me as words. I cross my eyes to push him out of focus. When none of this works to block him out I release my thighs, letting them go slack, then take my hands off the branches. I hit the ground. I am not dead.

His dogs bark and circle me as if I am a wounded animal shot at close range. These same dogs get him out of the house, provide him with a place to go. Walks in the woods keep him from the playgrounds, from the slides and swings and monkey bars, from finding a girl's voice to follow. If the mothers knew this was why their daughters were safe, they would worship the dogs.

I am done, I tell him as I shake the leaves and dirt from my hair.

He drapes his coat over my shoulders. In the car he turns the heater to full blast.

Open the glove compartment. He says.

Inside is a gift for me. I rip open the wrapping paper. It's a stuffed animal, Dorothy's dog from *The Wizard of Oz*, a tiny Toto, a terrier with a pink ribbon tied around its neck.

◀ ◀ ◀

On Your Mark Get Set Go.
Maroon and white gym shorts rush across the field. I run in the opposite direction of my classmates, through woods, where at first there is a path, but as I go deeper and farther I am jumping over branches, leaves, piles of stone, a kitchen sink, the rusted hood of a car that was once blue, over a damp gully with moss-covered stones, a tumbled wall of rock, across tall grasses, to a place of mostly tree stumps.

I change course and head towards the sun. The white stripe of my gym suit is stained brownish-yellow from sweat and there is blood on my socks.

By now all the others are at home doing their schoolwork. Their mothers are cooking dinner and they are asking when it will be ready.

◀ ◀ ◀

The back doors of the Cadillac would be locked and the windows closed. Somewhere in the Bronx, Mother stiffened, paying close attention, telling Father which turn to take. He often exited the highway too soon, probably to cause Mother concern, or maybe because he saw how quiet and focused Helen and I became, as we studied the forbidden landscape of burned-out buildings and the seemingly endless blocks of rubble.

Men, mostly, congregated in the empty lots. In winter, fires burned in discarded barrels, the orange flame and black smoke moved menacingly above the rim of metal, threatening to envelope the faces and arms of those who bowed before them. The men did not step back to avoid the flame, but moved in closer.

In summer, the fireplugs were open at full force and children ran through the gushing water. Some kids were naked while others wore only underwear. I wanted Father to go deeper into this part of the city. It wasn't just the grit and grime but how real it was in comparison to the choreographed perfection of our suburban landscape: manicured lawns and evenly shorn hedgerows, carefully cleaned children, daffodils in spring, and snowmen in winter with raisin mouths that were always in the shape of a smile.

Leaning into mortar and brick, against a wall spray-painted in a wild swirl of red, stood men strung out on drugs, their eyes half-open, cigarettes hanging from bruised lips, sometimes one lit and one unlit. Helen pointed out the man with a green parrot on his shoulder and named the parrot Parrot Pete and the man Parrot Man. Years later I asked her if she had thought about Parrot Man and if she wondered if he had died. We agreed it was likely. Helen asked her teachers how long a parrot lives. We imagined Parrot Pete had been orphaned.

It was on a street where the traffic lights didn't work that Father stopped and parked the car in front of a windowless building with crumbling concrete steps. For Helen and me it was spectacular to be so close to one of the facades we had been watching for years, wondering what went on behind its walls, in hallways and rooms where we would never be allowed to go.

Even though it was warm outside, Mother insisted on keeping the windows up and the doors closed and locked. Father walked up the steps, avoiding the piles of garbage, and went inside. Mother was agitated and chewed her pinky finger even though she had recently sat for a manicure. Father came out of the building with a tall black man who was missing his front teeth. The man went to the left while Father opened the trunk of the car. The man returned, pushing a motorcycle that he then hoisted into the trunk. The car lurched forward from the weight. The motorcycle must have been stolen because Father never licensed it and only rode it on the streets of our neighborhood.

He promised us a ride as soon as we got home. The guy didn't sell Father helmets and Mother tried to insist we couldn't ride without one. Father was unsteady at first but when he got the feel of the bike, he took Helen for a ride in our neighborhood.

He said, Helen hold onto my waist and don't take your hands off me. Both hands, you get it?

She nodded.

They circled many times, passing the two-car attached garages, the lawns without trees, the black shutters on white clapboard fronts. Finally Jake got his turn.

I didn't want a turn. Father was annoyed. It wasn't that I had sided with Mother. It was that I was afraid.

◀ ◀ ◀

The first time I went to New York City by myself a friend told me which subway to take from Grand Central. All I carried was my portfolio. Other expectant photographers were seated on the floor waiting to be interviewed by the professor, hoping for a place in her master class. I fiddled with the laces of my portfolio, tying and untying knots. There were more applicants than spots and number two in line wanted us to think she knew the professor and therefore had an edge. I tried not to listen as she rattled off names of known photographers.

The professor's white shoulder-length hair was in stark contrast to her black dress that reached to the floor. She spent a long time on each of my photographs, turning them on their sides, even upside down, but didn't ask any questions.

My memory of the class is of the long table where the seven of us met. The professor was at the far end, sunken into her chair looking at photographs until she spoke, and then she righted her torso perfectly straight. She was direct but never cruel.

When it was my turn, I pinned my prints to the corkboard and stood beside them and answered questions. Sometimes the professor asked to see the contact sheet of the negatives. Of the ones I had decided weren't worthy of being printed, she said my judgment was sound.

Our last class was held at the Metropolitan Museum of Art in the hall of ancient Greek sculpture. I took a photograph of the professor against the outline of the marble discus thrower. He is in position, a split second before he releases the disc, but I have him slightly out of focus so the viewer is directed to look into the eyes of the professor, who stares at the camera, her eyes nearly burning through the film.

After each class I took a cab to Grand Central and rode the commuter train home. I was always on the 8:10 and Mother met me at the station at 9. A man in a suit and tie, his hard, black brief case with initials engraved in gold on the front of the case, sat predictably in the last seat of the first car. He gave me his phone number after we talked about photography. I said I could help him set up a darkroom. His number was in the spiral notebook I took to class and I did try, on a few occasions, to call him. The Photographer and I had been arguing.

A few years later I returned to the school to look for the professor. She died, the lady at the desk said.

I was unable to get a cab and wandered around looking for the subway entrance. With the portfolio leaning against my shins I looked for a Kleenex in my bag. I hadn't figured on the professor—although she was old and frail—dying. I needed the time to understand what she had asked me to consider, and then as it came to me, I needed to construct a way to express it. The finished project was in my portfolio, a series of self-portraits. Each photograph is a separate page in a book, bound between two pieces of heavy cardboard. I used black leather thread and one of Mother's heaviest sewing needles to make the cross-stitches.

In the first image I wear a ski suit, facemask and goggles.

Page two: a hazmat suit, hood and Plexiglas faceguard.

Page three: painter's coveralls, mask and work glasses.

Page four: hijab.

The section ends with me in a habit, veil and wimple.

Part II of the book is a photograph of each of the previous outfits without the subject, displayed on a mannequin in the middle of a wooded area taken on the shortest day in winter. I wedged Mother's Styrofoam head from her long-ago discarded fall onto the mannequin's neck to accommodate the head and face gear.

A man approached me. I asked him to direct me to the subway.

Are you okay? He asked. I am on my way to Brooklyn. To the botanical garden. Why don't you come?

There was an urgency to his request.

What's in your portfolio?

Photographs.

I love to look at photographs. You can show me in the garden.

Are you sure you are okay?

They are self-portraits.

I love photographs of women.

I realized I needed to get away. Maybe because I was older or maybe because of what was in my portfolio, I knew.

What would have happened if I had gone with this man to Brooklyn, how long would it have taken Mother and Father to realize that I disappeared?

◀ ◀ ◀

A young girl so thin it is difficult to tell her age sits underneath an umbrella. The man with her wears a tight bathing suit. His soot grey hair is haphazardly tucked behind his ears and curls at the nape of his neck. A cigarette hangs from her mouth. He leans over and takes it from her lips, shiny with sunscreen, inhales two times and returns it to her half-opened frown.

Behind me I hear the Photographer.

The girl stands when the bikinied man reaches over to touch her. On instinct she runs. He fumbles to get his sandals on. Then goes after her.

The Photographer motions to me.

I follow him.

Red wallpaper, red curtains, red rug. He sits down on the bed and pats the spot next to him, inviting me to sit. My eyes begin at his feet and work their way up from his malformed toes and calloused heels to his chest hairs, more white than brown. I am on my feet. I glance back to see if he is following, and even though I don't see him, I do not stop.

◀ ◀ ◀

The Photographer threads unexposed film into his camera. Over there, at that inlet, he says, is where I learned to swim.

He focuses on a bank of sand in the distance, and in this flat light it won't look like anything but a cardboard cutout. I try to walk away but he catches up to me, grabbing me from behind. I fall forward. He rolls me over and unzips my coat, unbuttons my shirt, then spreads my legs apart, pegging me beneath him. The dogs brush against us, shaking sand across our faces. Still, he doesn't stop. I stare at the eroded dune to my left and study the winter debris deposited across a layer of black silt. A faded pink plastic tampon insert is entwined in the knotty seaweed.

When he is done, he photographs me, sand imprinted in my skin, the drip of his saliva crusted on my cheek and the mess he has made between my legs. He will print these images and keep me there with him, watching me whenever he wants.

I go back alone and shimmy the legs of my tripod into the sand and photograph my naked torso, mimicking the way I must have looked when he pinned me there. I make a necklace with the seaweed and draw the torso of a girl in the sand using a piece of driftwood, no wider than a twig. At the neck I place the seaweed linked together to form a chain and adorn it with shells. The girl's face has no features and no expression.

A family is on the beach wrapped in winter coats and hats. The daughter takes photographs of the sun reflecting on the water, of her parents and brother, maybe of their scarfs that, like kites, fill with wind. I can't be sure if she photographs me but her camera is fitted with a telephoto lens. I wonder if her friends and family, when they flip through her photo album, ask who I am. Or can they see I am nothing more than a prop?

◄ ◄ ◄

Most nights Helen isn't home but tonight she's on our bed with a magazine. Her clothing is everywhere. Spilled across the surface of the dresser are the insides of her pocketbook.

Don't lift your head above the window ledge, I tell her. He's still out there, I'm sure of it, in the shrubs, focusing, getting ready to shoot.

She gets up and pulls the blinds down.

No, Helen, I mean it. I point at the blouse I am wearing. It's ruined, ripped sideways, not even along a seam. He did it. I toss it at her.

At least he gives you good gifts and has a car and pays for things. She says, as she examines the shirt. I'm going for ice cream, want some?

He pulled me by my hair. The more he yanked the more I resisted. Back and forth until his hand slipped. That's when he grabbed the shirt.

Helen lights a cigarette butt. Just a small tear, you probably walked into something. Are you sure, no ice cream? Mother bought chocolate.

The third and fifth stair creak. They have always served as a warning. Father's step makes a particularly deep groan. Had Helen not left at that moment I might have said I was sorry for having told on her. For exaggerating what I knew, even making things up, for all the trouble I hoped she would get into, for wanting her to get caught. I wanted Mother to approve of me, and thought she would, if she compared me to Helen. I would apologize for looking more like Father. It's the only reason I can think of as to why he passed me over.

◀ ◀ ◀

The Photographer works in the dark, manipulating the shadows, reconfiguring my image, staring at me as I emerge from the red plastic pans filled with chemicals. He moves my head to another person's body, dangles it from a tree branch. A composite of many shots of my breasts and arms are woven together, forming what looks like a garden hose of coiled snakes, one on top of the other. Only the last snake is different. It has turned its head counterclockwise as it tries to swallow itself.

Father looks through the scope of his automatic rifle. Helen's head is centered between the crosshairs. When he is done visualizing the kill, he will go to the woods. What he catches he will gut before cutting it into smaller pieces to be wrapped and saved in freezer paper. There will be no room in the freezer for our chocolate ice cream.

In Father's hunting bag he keeps two books. *Slash & Thrust* and *The Semiautomatic Pistol in Police Service and Self-Defense.*
Father underlined, "To apply a cut or thrust, it is necessary to have a practical knowledge of human anatomy. There are several arteries that if severed will cause death in less than a minute" He has made an asterisk at this passage and underlined three times. "Wounds that cause death in ten seconds or less are called quick kills."

I would like the hunter to wake up. To be groggy enough to mistake the Photographer for a prowler. I give him a meager wave of goodbye. He takes the corner too close and the tires of his van rub against the curb.

◀ ◀ ◀

Father stops the car at the end of the driveway. He should be at work and Helen should be in school. Mother is the first to get out. She walks towards the front door, holding her patent leather pocketbook close to her chest. I cannot tell from my window why Helen is not moving. Father doesn't seem to be talking to her. He hasn't changed position, not even turned his head.

Eventually Helen pushes the seat forward and gets out. She is unsteady as she begins to walk. Her skirt is badly creased. She is wearing her leather jacket that she never takes off at home, but I know from school she wears tight tee shirts light in color beneath it and no bra. I can see that she did not take the time to iron her hair as she does each morning. Instead she has pulled it into a loose braid, which is now messy and nearly undone.

As she passes me in the foyer, she says to Mother. I had nothing to do with this. Why don't you ask Daddy?

Her black eyeliner has stained her cheeks and her eyes are red and swollen. She leaves a thin trail of blood on the wooden floor. I want to ask if she is okay or if there is something I can do, but she closes and locks her bedroom door before I have a chance. She doesn't come out all night, not even to use the bathroom.

The blood on the floor upsets me so I take a wad of wet toilet paper and wipe it. It has already started to harden around the edges. I throw the paper into the toilet, and as it spreads apart and the color drains from it, I think there is quite a lot of blood.

I don't think Father came home all night and he isn't here when we wake up, which is why Mother let Helen sleep in, missing her first three periods.

She is never pregnant again, even though, later in life, she wants to have a child.

◀ ◀ ◀

A policeman brings Jake home. Is your mother here?
My brother's shoes and pants are caked in mud.

Only my older sister and she isn't well enough to come downstairs. Mother will be back in a few minutes.

Has she been gone long?

She's driving the maid to the train.

Is this your brother?

Yes, sir.

Jake tries to scrape the mud from his pant leg but makes it worse because his sneakers are even dirtier.

He and the boy next door, I just left the other one with his mother, were throwing rocks at the ducks. Your neighbor, he points across the street, reported it. She said this isn't the first time, although she wasn't sure if your brother was involved in the incident last month.

Jake interrupts: It was an accident. He shifts his weight and doesn't look up from the floor where dirt is accumulating.

I know I will have to clean this mess up before Mother gets back, that Jake won't help. If the policeman were to come inside, he would bang his head on the foyer fixture made of crystals that cascade from a center cylinder. His pants are tucked into his ankle boots making him look very tall. He wears a wooden stick that hangs from his belt and hits his left thigh when he shifts position. I try not to look curious but I am sure he is carrying a pistol in his holster.

One of them, he says, killed the duck. Not sure which one. They both deny it.

Helen and I never let Jake play with our baby ducks, only look. We might have allowed it when he got older but we didn't get to keep them that long. It had been Helen's idea to strap the ducklings' box into Jake's old baby carriage. We paraded through the neighborhood, wanting the other children to see us and beg for a turn to push the carriage or for a chance to hold one. They were little soft cotton balls that made a beautiful squeaking sound. Midway, Helen let me steer. I didn't have to ask.

When Mother said we weren't taking care of the ducks properly, she took them and left them at the pond closest to the elementary school. Helen begged Mother to let us rescue them. When Mother refused, we walked to the pond ourselves. It took us all afternoon to get there and back. But they weren't there. Maybe Mother sold them to the butcher. She would never have fed them to us. We didn't eat duck. Just chicken.

The policeman writes a phone number on a piece of paper in his spiral notebook before ripping out the page and handing it to me. Make sure your mother calls when she gets home. When I think the policeman is finished, I close the door slowly in case he wants to say something else.

When the policeman is at the end of the walk, I call to Jake, who is on his way upstairs, was it really an accident?

I bring Helen her tea, which is what I was doing before the doorbell rang, and start to tell her about the duck.

She says, you kept me waiting all this time and now the tea isn't even hot. Get me the heating pad, and when Mother gets back, don't have her park the car, tell her she is going to have to take me to the hospital. I am dying.

◀ ◀ ◀

There is an old desk pushed against the wall in the garage where Father keeps his tools. In late fall I open the top drawer looking for a hammer. I scream and run inside, it isn't just the smell, but the decayed frog parts, an entire desk drawer stuffed full.

Maybe the frogs went into the drawer in search of food. Maybe their deaths hadn't been intentional.

They were gone the next day. Even the smell. Maybe I made it up.

◀ ◀ ◀

Before I open the car door I smell fish. The Photographer parks under an elevated train line, a rusty, blackened structure where discarded plastic bags dangle, caught on sharp edges. The cobblestone streets are uneven and water runs between the stones even though it hasn't been raining.

We walk a few blocks. There are no streetlights and no car lights, only the glow before us. Men in white aprons with huge rubber boots shuttle fish, sometimes two or three men to a single fish, into parked trucks laden with ice.

Inside, under light bulbs and long florescent tubes, I see the men's aprons, not white anymore, but the color of blood. Fresh red stains, some seeming as if they are still bleeding alongside the older, darker stains that are more brown than red. The fish are so recently dead their eyes are still gelatinous. I think they can see me.

All the tiny neon scales coalesce into circles of light, brighter than the overhead bulbs. Men scale the fish, while others cut through the length of the underbellies, slopping the innards into plastic bags, while there are still other vendors who leave their fish whole. So many carcasses are piled on the floor it is difficult to walk.

The men stare at me. I am sorry I am not wearing a bra and my thin tee shirt makes me feel naked. I look down. The drains in the floor are clogged with fish guts.

They don't want us photographing them. A guy with a long dagger-like knife tells the Photographer to leave. The Photographer starts to argue with him but catches himself. On our way out I pass a table where the fish are still squirming, very much alive, gasping, unable to battle it out much longer now that the water is gone.

◄ ◄ ◄

The siren is getting closer. I see red lights flash, reflecting on a pane of glass. Two men push a stretcher down the front path to our door where Mother is waiting.

Mother points upstairs.

When the men come down, I see a pile of hair at the top of the stretcher. Helen is covered by a hospital-issued blanket and an intravenous bag hangs on a silver hoop above her head. A black band for taking blood pressure is secured around her upper arm. Mother doesn't take her coat or Helen's even though it is winter and there is snow on the ground.

Jake and I stand and watch the ambulance leave. Then he turns and walks up the stairs. I follow holding onto the fabric of his striped green and blue shirt. I imagine the red blood spots that had once dotted the hallway floor, but this time much larger, more like puddles of blood.

Jake goes into Helen's room and picks up a glass pipe, moving the tiny screen on top of the bulb. Small white pebbles fall to the floor. Science stuff, he says.

Album covers and LPs are strewn across the carpet.

Don't touch anything. I tell him. Just leave it the way it is.

Let's get out of here, he says. I'm hungry.

Jake sits at his place at the kitchen table in front of Mother's bowl of plastic fruit. Helen was first to pull off the grapes and suction them onto her tongue. She held them there, and when she used her teeth to release them, they made a slurping sound. Jake and I copied her, liking how it felt and the sound. We thought it funny until Father lost his temper, and when Helen didn't stop laughing, it only made him angrier. So angry, he took the bowl and moved it off the table and slammed it onto the counter.

I wanted it to break. I wanted him to see it shatter into so many tiny shards of glass that it could not be pieced together and glued back into place. Now the bare stalks make the other fruit look especially fake.

I fidget with the plastic apples, which include one yellow and one red. Coco chewed the green one into sections a long time ago, and it wasn't possible to replace just one. They were sold in groups of three.

Jake gets up and takes a bag of cookies from the cupboard and goes into the TV room and turns on *The Flintstones*. After *The Flintstones*, comes *The Jetsons* and in the middle of *The Jetsons* the phone begins to ring. Neither of us moves. It rings again.

It is my Father's secretary, but she never calls the house.

Are you and Jake okay?

Yes. Thank you.

Your Father is on his way to Grand Central. When he gets off the train, he will go directly to the hospital, it's where your mother and Helen are.

His secretary isn't married and she doesn't have experience with kids.

What's wrong?

An accident with Helen.

Is she okay?

I don't know. I guess she will be. Can you get a piece of paper and write down my phone number?

Why?

In case you need something.

More rings during *Bewitched*. This time it is my Grandmother. I ask about Helen. She says she doesn't know anything.

The next morning before Mother is out of bed, the maid cleans Helen's room, putting her albums in the wrong sleeves and lining her shoes across the ledge of her closet floor. One pair is missing the right foot, which seems like a nearly impossible thing to do, lose one shoe, especially because Helen prefers shoes to anything else. When the maid puts the comforter across Helen's bed, I run and get Mother.

Where is she and why are you making her room look perfect? Is company coming?

With everything that is going on?

But what is going on? Maybe she doesn't know how to say Helen is dead.

She's in New Hampshire near where Jake goes to camp.

At camp?

No, not at camp.

How come we didn't get a chance to see her before she left and why didn't she take her things?

Where she is, it's good.

When I look through Helen's room, which I do frequently because I am afraid she isn't coming back, I look for clues.

I ask Jake if he thinks she's dead.

The only thing missing, he says, is her baby blanket, which they could have buried her with.

But all her other things that she couldn't be without are where she left them: the white-colored lipsticks and black mascara, her clothing—except now these things are perfectly aligned and the tops and covers are in place.

Have you looked today? Jake asks. It is all gone. Dad threw everything out. He was stuffing a huge trash bag, the kind he puts leaves in before he burns them in the gutter. And when he was finished, he locked her door. I didn't know it could be locked from the outside.

On Saturday, Father burns the bag. The smoke rises from the backyard and curls over the roof of our house, turning the morning sky from a clear blue to clouds of black and then dull gray. The fire doesn't smell crisp and fresh the way leaves do, but acrid and heavy and hangs above us until the afternoon wind picks up and carries off the soot and the smell. While he's outside, I hear the china in the kitchen moving across the table. Mother is setting and resetting the table.

One week after Helen leaves, Mother returns to her schedule. Father hasn't missed a day of work. I want to think that they would not be in their routine if Helen were dead.

◀ ◀ ◀

It's not that I miss Helen. It's that I'm afraid I might have had something to do with her being sent away. I took pleasure telling on her. And now I am convinced I will be next.

I pack a few things in a grocery bag and store it under my bed, this way all I have to do when they come is grab the bag, taking my stuffed yellow mouse and red blanket. I don't want these things to be left behind to be burned by Father.

Mother is calmer without Helen at home. At night Father doesn't roam the house. When he travels to Europe, he brings me an Eiffel Tower from Paris filled with cologne. For Jake he brings a matchbox car. There is nothing for my sister and she has always been his favorite.

Helen's boyfriend, the one Mother approves of because his father is well known in town, is at the front door holding a life-sized teddy bear. There is a card in a red envelope tied around the bear's neck. He hands it to Mother. I was hoping you could get this to Helen.

We can't visit, Mother says, so for now I'll put it in her room for when she comes home.

◀ ◀ ◀

Mother is cooking lamb for dinner. It's Helen's favorite. She asks me to set the table for five.

A white van pulls up. The driver walks my sister to the front door. She is thin, dressed in grey pants and a ski jacket that is too large, especially in the arms. I have never seen these clothes. Before Helen went away, she never would have worn a ski jacket or pants that were not jeans. Mother takes the brown bag Helen carries and steps to the side so Helen can come in. She doesn't take Helen in her arms or kiss her.

Jake comes downstairs. Hi, he says.

Helen pats his head.

Mother asks him to take the grocery bag into the laundry room and unload it directly into the washing machine. After washing her hands she turns to Helen, who hasn't moved from the doorway, and asks if she would like something to drink.

No, thank you.

Maybe a shower? Your Father won't be home for at least an hour.

Helen shakes her head no. Then walks into the den and turns on the television. She doesn't take off the ski jacket. The television is on the nightly news channel my parents watch after dinner. At this hour the news is local. There are reports of stolen swings from the playground, a disease that is killing the elms, and the garbage men are threatening to go on strike. Helen doesn't change the channel even though I am sure these things do not interest her and she doesn't lower the volume, which is too loud.

Mother has no reason to be in the kitchen. Dinner is prepared, the table is set, the mail is in an orderly pile at Father's place setting.

I don't feel relief that Helen is back. I peer over my dinner of lamb stew and green mint jelly that Mother serves in the same glass container it is packaged in. Jake and I hate this meal. One of us will get yelled at for moving our food around to make it look as if we have eaten. I try to force myself to finish some of the meat, but when the fork gets close to my mouth I gag. I know if I throw up, it will be even worse.

Helen says, please pass the salt. Then, Thank you.

She puts on too much salt the way she always has. Mother catches herself just as she is about to tell Helen she has added enough, that salt isn't a food but a spice, which means use it sparingly. Usually Helen rolls her eyes but keeps on shaking. This happens at every dinner, and at breakfast when there are eggs.

A few more words are exchanged about the color of the napkins and what is in the stack of mail. My stomach is hurting and we aren't even halfway into the meal. We chew our food and wipe our mouths and reach for the water glasses to our right, and when our plates are empty, we know that the part of dinner that is lamb is now over.

Finally Mother serves dessert. It is three-layered Jell-O in red. The first layer is regular Jell-O, then a foamy Jell-O, followed by custard-like Jell-O. Each layer tastes the same. It is the texture that is different and the foamy one is the worst. It sticks to my teeth and makes it difficult to swallow.

Father's blob of Jell-O plops off his spoon just before it reaches his mouth and bounces off his tie.

Jake laughs.

Mother shoots Jake a nasty look.

It's the Jell-O. Jake can barely get the words out he is laughing so hard. He uses his spoon and has it jump up and down across the surface as if it is a red trampoline. Helen doesn't join him, although the old Helen definitely would have done something even funnier.

Father tucks his tie into his still crisp white work shirt. Usually he takes his suit jacket off but he is still wearing it as if there is something special about this night, Helen being home.

Mother says to Jake, that's enough. And to me, Leslie, you and Jake will clean up.

My parents get up and walk in the direction of the den. Before he has pushed his chair under the table, Father has nodded to Helen to follow. I am sorry for her—that she has to be with them alone—yet she goes without making a fuss. She must want to scream, or push herself into the wall, or scratch her fingernails across the paint, maybe drag her shoes over the polished wooden floor, but she doesn't do any of this, she just walks in a straight line following them.

Jake tiptoes from the kitchen and hovers outside the den door to try and hear what they are saying. When he comes back he cannot tell me anything.

◀ ◀ ◀

For Helen it was the cheese sandwich.

Years later I ask and she says she doesn't remember a cheese sandwich, or ever having mentioned one.

Mother was getting her hair done. Father was supposed to drive you to Janie Battle's after lunch. You were probably eleven. Cheese made you gag and you didn't want the sandwich. What you told me was you wrapped it in a napkin, and when Father wasn't looking, you took it into the powder room and buried it in the wicker trash can underneath a mound of tissues. But you hesitated when you were telling the story because you weren't sure. You said maybe he planted the sandwich just to get you in trouble, so he would have reason to punish you. You also said it didn't matter if you had buried it or if he had, because if it hadn't been the sandwich it would have been something else, just so he could keep you home with him. You don't remember telling me this?

You mean the white wicker trash can that had pale blue ribbons laced through the thatch? The ends of the ribbons were sewn together with clear white buttons, that one?

Yes. I think it was in Jake's nursery for a while.

It was. Mother made it for him before he was born. I remember helping her pick out the buttons. I remember that trash can. But the cheese sandwich?

◀ ◀ ◀

On Long Island Sound, maybe City Island, definitely not Manhattan, were they friends of his—the ones with the sailboat? I don't know if it was moored or if it was at a slip or how we got to it. Maybe a dingy or a launch. Practically everything is forgotten except the end of the night car ride. Did we sail or just drink? How big was the boat, where did we sit and what did we say?

The Photographer ordered me to get into the driver's seat. I never drove when I was with him. It was warm out or else I didn't mind the temperature, no it was something close to summer.

I had way too much to drink. I tell him.

So have I. I can direct you.

Direct me?

I will tell you how to do it.

I can't see, not clearly. Just lights. That's it and they are blurring everything. Is it raining? Coffee. That would be best, coffees for everyone. Or we should sleep here in the car. Back or front?

He grabs me and drags me by my arm and opens the driver's side door and pushes me into the seat. We aren't sleeping here.

No, really. I drool. Can't, not happening. Can't do this, not tonight.

The Photographer is in the passenger seat. I'm gonna tell you exactly what to do.

You can't see either. You just said, I can't see. Oh God, forgive me I peed my pants. I can't drive wet. Did we drink beer? What a lot of piss.

Somehow I got us to the parkway. I remember him saying okay, now, and that's when I would switch lanes. But this is all I remember. Not the road. Where I drove us. Where we spent the night.

◄ ◄ ◄

Preferring woods and not wanting neighbors nearby, Father buys a summer house on Lake George. The phone and television work intermittently.

I hear Helen's shoeless feet inching up the wooden stairs at the same time the sun is rising. Mother no longer draws attention to her absences.

Helen's friend comes to visit and they lie naked on the flat roof outside Helen's window, stretched across a sheet of foil that reflects the sun, aluminum visors resting on their bony chests. They squeeze lemon into their hair, wincing from the tartness as it runs into their torn cuticles. Then, with both hands, they spread the pulp through each other's scalps, hoping this will give them streaks of blonde. When it doesn't work fast enough, they add hydrogen peroxide, which turns their hair orange. The upstairs bathroom smells of baby oil and the floor is slippery.

Sunday evening before Father leaves, he forbids Helen to continue sunning on the roof. He tells her he has seen them out there all weekend, that their weight will loosen the shingles and then, after a winter of freezing and a spring of thawing, the roof will leak.

She rolls her eyes. I imagine her turning sickly green, like the moss that grows in splotches on the flat stones outside my window.

◄ ◄ ◄

We, Mother included, follow Father single file to the dock. A wooden board straddles both sides of a narrow creek. As I am about to step onto the plank, a thick black snake slithers underneath. I stand perfectly still and don't want to move until it is gone, but Father is impatient and tells me to keep moving. Helen takes my hand. Now he is angry with both of us, but says to Helen, leave her, she knows how to walk by herself.

I hold Helen's hand.

As we walk, I study Mother. Her skirt is neat and pressed, hemmed at the knee, not even one stray thread hangs. The periwinkle cashmere set she is wearing matches perfectly. Her blood red nail polish is not chipped. I want her to do anything to turn things around, jump into the water fully dressed, or take her clothes off and then jump in, so that maybe Father will do something differently.

Mother bends her knees, holding her skirt to keep it from riding up her thighs. Lips pursed, she climbs into the boat.

Jake is happy for the ride. Father likes to speed and challenges any nearby boat to race. Mother, Helen, and I hold the metal railing with clenched fists, our knuckles turning white. Mother begs Father to slow down, saying her hair is a mess, that she has forgotten her comb. From her lacquered wicker pocketbook shaped like a lunch box with a metal clasp affixed to a leather flap, she takes out a scarf and fights the wind, but is unable to position it evenly on her head. The speed of the boat makes our eyes tear. Mascara leaks down Mother's cheeks.

Helen's head is tucked into her chest and she huddles on the fiberglass floor. I crouch down next to her and stare at her jacket zipper that, when it catches the sunlight, glistens.

64

We sit on the couch that faces the television, even though it is off, and fidget. The grown-ups are across the way, drinking different-colored cocktails. No one touches the food on the table. Even from where I am sitting, I can see the red insides of the olives and the plastic toothpicks tightly packed into a rectangular holder. Helen is expert at dissecting food, and although I have never seen her work on olives, I imagine she would coax the red tails from their middles and line them off to the side before squishing the greasy green skin flat. The pimentos would be the pool of blood and the green casings would be men in camouflage.

Every Valentine's Day, Father gets angry with Helen because she sticks her finger into the chocolates, starting in on them from the bottom, excavating the insides to determine what they are made of, and after investigating the filling by feel and scent and sometimes taste, she reconstructs them as they once were to make it seem as if they had never been touched. We are usually fooled, and even though we try not to, we end up selecting one of hers, but it isn't until we bite down and find the cavity empty that we know for sure.

Mother's eyes are dull and she isn't talking, not even in short sentences, or in reply. Mrs. Jones interrupts and calls across the room to ask us if we want to play Parcheesi. We don't know what this is but Father tells us to follow her into the family room where the games are stored.

Once she's gone Jake wants to play Hangman because it's a game he thinks he can win. We find a pencil and some loose sheets of paper. I draw the gallows and seven dashes. Five guesses later, he has only one letter and I have hung his head and neck, and torso. He wants to quit, because like Father, he hates to lose.

Mrs. Jones is at the door and announces dinner is being served. I am embarrassed the Parcheesi board isn't open, but she doesn't seem to notice. Once a year we are invited to the same dinner where we are fed something Mr. Jones has shot. It is prepared exactly like last year's meal, a slab of meat in a shiny sauce that is, by the time we get served, hard at the edges. The peas and carrots are piled neatly on one side of the plate. There are more carrots than peas. Father normally doesn't eat carrots. He says they are poor people's food, but at the Jones', all of us must eat what we are served.

Jake and I struggle to get each bite down, washing our mouths with gulps of milk until Mother summons the housekeeper who is wearing a white tufted cap and a matching white pressed apron. She tells her not to bring us any more milk. She doesn't like it when we make that gulping sound or when we throw our heads back to make the meat go down. Without the milk we won't be able to do it, which forces us to fill our napkins with unchewed meat and then we must guard the napkins so when the maid clears them away the meat doesn't fall to the floor. We manage to get them into the bathroom and flush them down the toilet, or into the kitchen trash by pretending we are well-mannered and clear our places even though there is a staff.

We want to go home but the adults are drinking liquor that smells like licorice. Mother tries to catch Father's eye to signal that it is time to go, but he doesn't acknowledge her. After what seems a very long time, Mr. and Mrs. Jones walk us to their private dock where our boat is tied. Helen refuses to take the seat next to Father and he is too drunk to protest. He zigzags the boat across the lake at high speed and when he steps away from the wheel and makes it seem as if we are going to crash, both he and Jake find it so funny.

◀ ◀ ◀

There is blood at Coco's mouth and something bulging at both sides of her neck. Father tells me to get into the back seat of his car. Hurry, he says, it is a long drive. The nearest vet is far away and we don't have much time. Father lifts Coco and places her head on my lap.

How far is it really?

We don't have time to get Mother. Two hours at least.

She won't make it, will she?

Keep her head elevated. She's having trouble breathing.

I stare out the back window at a bog covered in green sludge. I now know it was only algae, but at the time I was sure it was a disease that would spread to the surrounding area, engulfing the healthy trees and plants, eventually taking over the forest.

Mother went alone to the pet store after a neighbor told her they were selling off a litter of brown poodles with a perfect pedigree. Mother had already decided on Coco because when we went with her later in the week we weren't allowed to play with any of the other puppies. On Saturday she brought Father and convinced him to buy the dog. Mother named her, took her to training class and let her sleep in her bed when Father was away.

Father stays with Coco until the vet takes her into the operating room. He comes outside to tell me she is in surgery. Why don't you get out of the car?

No. I'm afraid.

Of what? He asks impatiently.

He turns away and goes back inside for what seems a very long time. I wait in the back seat with the door open.

Eventually Father comes outside. Let's go, he says and slams my door, then his.

On the drive home I see bubbles forming on the swamp's oily surface. I count the green circles as they ripple towards the shore, certain they belong to someone being dragged down, struggling to find her last breath.

Mother sits on the kitchen floor in front of the cabinet under the sink where she keeps Coco's bowls. She is crying quietly and I can see her hands are shaking as she holds Coco's favorite toy, a squirrel that squeaks. Helen painted Coco on her two metal bowls, using a bright pink waterproof paint. Mother untangles two leashes, the short one with a handle studded with diamond-shaped rhinestones used on fancy occasions and the everyday one. The rawhide treats are next, the plastic lunch bag with three bottles of pills and the Tupperware container filled with enough kibbles to last the summer. To her left is a garbage bag, the kind Father likes to burn. Before she notices me I turn and walk away.

When the Photographer's black dog is dying he swaddles it in a blanket and carries it to his van. I take a photograph of them. The only visible part of the Photographer is his freckled hands. The sky is cloudy and there are no trees in the background, no way to identify where it was taken, or what season.

After a while the door to the vet's office opens and a different man hands the Photographer an urn. He sits on the curb and cries, but not for long.

The remaining dog, the all-white one, will sleep under the six urns that sit on his mantelpiece. A new dog will be in his house by the end of the week. It will smell as badly as the old dog and sleep on his bed, leaving a wide wet circle in the sheets.

◀ ◀ ◀

The farmer's son's front teeth were knocked out in a fight. His hair is longer than any girl's. Helen thinks everything about him is sexy. To me it looks as if he rarely bathes. All the rich summer kids buy their drugs from him but Helen says he saves the best for her. His family doesn't live in the summer compound, but on the other side of the highway, the last holdouts refusing to sell to the developer.

From their front stoop they sell tomatoes and corn. Thick plastic sheeting is taped across their front window where a pane of glass should be. Father has forbidden Helen to visit, but when the farmer's son is in a motorcycle accident, it is Helen's name that appears in the paper because she called the ambulance.

The paper quotes her. "They left, just drove off. Two cars and another motorcycle. I went back to the bar and called for help."

Mother buries the local section in the trash, and even though Father yells at her for misplacing it, she insists she doesn't have it.

I hear my parents' voices, then Roadrunner, that beep beep sound he makes, the crash before he falls from the cliff, and even though I am not watching, I know he will come back singed and smoldering. I hear something heavy drop, a photo album or a book of the month club selection, and my parents' bedroom door opens. Maybe Father found the newspaper and realized Mother covered for Helen.

The click clack of Mother's heels on the steps.

The kitchen faucet sputtering air, then a torrent of water.

Her aluminum pan hitting the burner.

An empty echo. Maybe the release of the vacuum seal on canned tomato sauce.

A fork or knife pinging the linoleum.

Mother walking on the wooden floor in the direction of the stairs.

Her voice. Dinnertime.

I try humming over their arguing and Jake will, if he has to, talk to himself. We have no radios in our rooms.

I fall asleep with the pillows over my head, and when I wake, it is to use the bathroom. I don't know if they have been to sleep and reawakened or if they have been arguing all this time. Because I am afraid to go into the hallway, I empty the pencils from the mug on my desk and go into my closet where I have no trouble peeing into it. It belongs to Father and says in black letters, University of Chicago, School of Law 1952.

◀ ◀ ◀

All summer it is Mother and the three of us, except on weekends when Father is here. Mother doesn't speak to him during the week. The phone is a party line that we share with the other houses in the community. We eavesdrop on them and we are sure they do the same.

Father buys us a telescope so we can learn the northern sky, which we never do. Jake and I use it to look into people's houses. Helen is fascinated by the farmer's son's interest in the solar system and the Mayan calendar. He points out Cassiopeia's belt and tells me she is in love with herself. He and Helen take the telescope to the field at night and wait for a comet, or maybe it is a solar eclipse. When the telescope is no longer where we keep it, I presume Helen has traded it for drugs. It is a while before Father notices that it is missing. Enough time has passed, so when Helen tells him she has no idea where it is, she may not be lying.

There is one television channel and most nights all we see are black and white dots or lines that keep rolling. It makes Helen so angry she bangs on the set. The banging doesn't change a thing.

◀ ◀ ◀

Running, we let ourselves fall through the wooden planks of the decaying steamboat dock. An ankle or knee snags in a crossbar and stops us from dropping all the way into the water. Mother is not gentle when she gouges the splinters out, using the tip of a sewing needle. Jake waits until the end of the summer to show her his foot, which is now so swollen she has to help him from the car into the emergency room. She makes me come inside.

A man is tying a tourniquet onto my leg as pieces of me fall on the linoleum floor. The maid who pressed my jumper Monday mornings comes to sweep me up. She collects everything and says she will put me back together when she finds the time.

The lady next to me hands me my magazine. It slipped, she says, I think you're next.

No. I'm waiting for my brother. That's who is screaming.

It's the staples, she says, they use staples nowadays, for stitches. She uses her thumb and pointer finger to show me how long each one is.

◀ ◀ ◀

I dig the soles of my feet into the clay that covers the bottom of the lake, opening and closing my toes. The water clouds and from the waist down I am missing.

I carry the clay in the apron of my bathing suit to the boulders that separate the lake from the woods. Stanchions of birch trees hide me. Autumn is coming and some of the leaves are already turning color. I spread myself on my back across the warm flat rocks, rubbing clumps of wet clay onto my legs and arms. I peel it away after it hardens and cracks. My skin is parched and wrinkled. With the still-wet clay, I roll arms and legs and connect these to rectangular torsos and flattened heads.

My family begins to dry.

Birch bark peels horizontally. I use it as paper and list the names. When I am done, I tie the scroll with the vein of a leaf, and at the end of the day I stash the list with the dried figurines in the crook of a rock. When summer is over, I bury us deep in the soil, posting no marker.

◀ ◀ ◀

Jake and I have seen the escaped convict that lives in the woods behind our house. Late at night the convict goes to the lake to collect water. Even though we have seen him running towards the mountain and have told our parents, they do not let us sleep together or with the light on. I console Jake by reminding him Father is a perfect marksman, who knows how to kill, who has killed all kinds of animals and practiced on clay disks and shot at pictures of heads and torsos.

At the end of August when all of the families close their houses, when the last car pulls away, the convict comes out of the woods and selects the most remote cabin. He will live there until spring, sleeping in a little girl's bedroom beneath a heap of blankets, the crocheted ones the grandmothers make and the woolen ones stored in the cedar chests under layers of mothballs.

◄ ◄ ◄

The Photographer unscrews the metal top and pours me a tall glass of vodka. The metal seal on the bottle of bourbon cuts into the palm of my hand. Streaks of blood stain the side of my glass. When he goes upstairs for a Band-Aid I submerge my bleeding hand into the glass of bourbon I poured him. The blood rises from the center of the oily liquid like the lava of a volcano. The streaks of blood intertwine and eventually thin out into slow-moving spirals.

Get your hand out of my drink.

It's a way to sterilize. It isn't more than a few drops of blood.

I was going to drink that.

You still can. I dare you.

You're crazy.

Do you think the blood will have the same effect in vodka? Or will it blend in, turning pink?

He grabs his bourbon and brings it into the grimy kitchen with a floor that shoeless feet stick to. From the cupboard he takes another glass and fills it to the top, swigging it down in a few gulps.

Let's go. He says. Get your coat.

He is driving south toward New York City. Out of habit and when I don't have anything else to do I smoke the cigarettes that are in the glove compartment. I am lighting one off the other as we cross the bridge into Riverdale.

He parks the car in Times Square.

Why here? I hate the lights, the ugliness.

There is a good restaurant. French.

If you'd asked I would've told you I'm not hungry.

He takes me by the arm and walks me three long, crosstown blocks to a movie theater.

I thought we were eating?

You just said you weren't hungry. Two tickets, he tells the man on the opposite side of the Plexiglas window and pushes a ten-dollar bill through the half-moon opening.

It's a porn flick. Of nurses dressed in cheap Halloween costumes, similar to what Helen's nurse doll and mine came dressed in, with the tri-cornered hats. Mother gave them to Helen and me when Jake was born. Helen liked her doll because it was nearly life-size, which is exactly why I didn't. The doll was too much work to dress and lug around. I didn't want mine, but pretended it was fine.

I try not to touch the armrest. I do not take off my coat. Every one in the theater is a man who is wearing either a hood or a woolen cap.

I lean over and whisper. I think we should leave.

A few more minutes, he says.

I sit with my eyes closed. Please, hasn't it been a few more minutes? I need to get out of here.

We are the only ones who leave midway.

It is cold outside. This I remember vividly, the way I was shivering, in a shaking sick sort of way, the body's response after retching.

◀ ◀ ◀

Father's father dies wedged between the toilet and the tub. His body spills into the spaces between the porcelain fixtures. At the end of his life his morning bathroom ritual took over three hours and included the reading of the Miami Herald, the Chicago Tribune and the Wall Street Journal. Not until noon, when he stacked them on the side table at the front door, was anyone allowed to read them. Grandmother never did, not even to flip through to look at the advertisements. Her job regarding the newspapers was to tie them with leftover red and white string from the bakery and carry them to the trash bin behind the house.

No one used his bathroom. Grandmother went in only to make sure he had not run out of products, to check that the towels were not damp or soiled and to ensure that the next Kleenex in the box had been threaded through. Hours later when Father arrives, Grandmother is still holding his now dry loofa.

It took some time for the EMS to extract him. Once he was on the stretcher they declared him dead. She had no choice but to let them take him from the house naked, covered only by the hospital sheet. There wasn't any blood to mop, only water. The neighborhood kids were playing in the street and didn't stop shouting, not even when they saw Grandmother crying as the men lifted the stretcher into the back of the ambulance. He had argued with them, the way they left their things scattered throughout the neighborhood and for all the noise they made.

Grandmother is waiting for Grandfather outside his bathroom door. She is holding his towel. She tells Father she has been doing this every night for as long as she can remember. If I am not here, she pauses, and something is missing, he doesn't like to have to call for me. The house is too big. So instead I just got in the habit of waiting to avoid the yelling.

Father brings Grandmother two tablets of Valium and a juice glass filled with cognac and leads her from Grandfather's bathroom door into the bedroom. She slumps in her chair with one foot on the ground and the other on the corner of the table. I know now she doesn't believe he is in the room or that he is coming back because if she did she would never have placed her foot there, he would scream if he caught her or anyone else mistreating the furniture.

Helen sleeps with Grandmother. She wants to see the dead man's ghost, which Grandmother insists will appear. I don't remember why I shared the room with Mother and why Jake was with Father and can only guess my parents had argued about something, and it wouldn't have been Helen because she was on her best behavior. My left shoe is missing and I get on my hands and knees to look for it under the bed. When I come up, I ask Mother why she didn't protect us. But she is asleep.

Grandmother makes pancakes for breakfast, and because she is in mourning, we can't tell her we don't want them. When we were little she told us stories of how she cooked breakfast for her family. She was the eldest and helped her mother with all her brothers and sisters, and if her father needed her, she would tend to the pigs and chickens. She was describing the pigpen and something reminded her of the time her father showed her how to drown a litter of kittens. He asked her to get the burlap sack and empty the oats and then to bring the kittens. All of them, he said, but don't touch them. The trick is to not know them. He held the bag open while she tipped the corner of the box into the sack.

There were seven plopping sounds as each one fell but only one made a high-pitched whine.

Tie it, he said.

But she didn't have any string.

Like this, he took the bag that was moving and twisted the neck to make a knot. She knew they could still breathe through the weave of the sack. Go fill the trough, he ordered, the one out back near the pigpen. All the way to the top.

I wanted to ask if she knew why she was running the water, but she had to have known. I wondered if she had been afraid that she might not have been able to do what he wanted, or had she remembered the color of each kitten or some other detail like the way the ears formed perfect triangles on their tiny heads, or was it just a chore like all the others?

When the trough was full, he took the bag and plunged it into the water. She watched it move. He held it submerged with both of his gigantic hands and when the bag stopped pulsating he pulled the dripping sack out of the water and carried it to the woods. He didn't make her follow. All she saw was the back of him, the shovel he carried, and the trail of water from the dripping bag. He returned from the edge of the woods with an empty sack.

When it dries, he said, put the oats back.

She took the bag and laid it across a flat boulder to dry and walked back to the house to watch her brothers and sisters.

Later in the day she prepared dinner, which was difficult because there was so little food. There wasn't meat so she made a soup of potatoes and onions even though her father hated only soup and cursed the children, they were responsible, all of them, so many of them, for why he could not afford meat.

The milk Grandmother pours into our pancake batter comes out in clots. She adds the other ingredients. I start to interrupt her to tell her the milk is spoiled but Father tells me to be quiet and stands over us to make sure that we stay that way, expecting that we will eat the pancakes as if we do not know they have been prepared with rotten milk. She doesn't offer Father any, but had she, he would have eaten his share. We manage to get them into the trash when she isn't looking.

Grandmother shows me a book of photographs from when Father was a boy. The corners of the glossy pictures are held in place by tiny gold triangles. Father stands alone, a stick-like figure positioned dead center in front of a white house. His eyes show no connection with the person taking the photograph.

Whose dog is that?

Your Father's.

I didn't know he had a dog.

He didn't have him long. Not even a week. When I realized the dog was no longer breathing he wouldn't let go, but pulled Rusty—that was the dog's name—closer to his chest, tucking his chin over the dog's head. Grandfather had to struggle with him to free the dog.

Why didn't you get him another?

I took him to Mass. I was afraid. You know your Grandfather worked on Sundays.

Did he mind you going to church?

He never said.

Was it the church your family went to?

No. They didn't live in Chicago.

Don't you miss them, especially now, maybe they should be here at the funeral?

Did you know that your Father was an altar boy and a bar mitzvah?

Helen and I leave for the airport after the funeral. I return to college and Helen goes back to her apartment. Father gives each of us a fifty-dollar bill, more money than he has ever given me. I accept it without hesitation. I think of it as a tip for not making a fuss about the pancakes, the sleeping arrangements, and for doing what was expected at the funeral. I wondered if Helen thought the same, but he had been giving her money for a very long time and I imagined that by now she was accustomed to even larger sums.

◄ ◄ ◄

Traveling, Helen and I need a room with a door that locks. The first place has no windows and a wooden bunk bed. I don't remember if there were mattresses because we didn't stay. I would have taken it just so we didn't have to keep looking. We no longer could figure out where we were on our map and Helen had used the bottom portion for toilet paper.

Helen had come a week earlier. The idea to permanently leave the country occurred to her in our childhood bedroom, and once she located the name of the town on the map, she decided it was where she was going to live. Named for a male saint, it is a tiny dot in the middle of Mexico. She had been staying in a place where the air conditioning unit in the window was at street level. Her neck is still stiff. But this isn't why she checked out. She was afraid anyone could remove the air conditioner from the outside and climb into her room.

Eventually we find our way to a better neighborhood. The room is adequate and the door locks. Cold water comes out of the shower but Helen is mostly distraught over how hot it is. She positions the only fan in the room so the breeze hits her face directly without asking me if I mind not being in the path of air.

Ever since we shared a room as teenagers we never turned out all the lights. Helen moved out of her room and insisted on sleeping in mine. I hated her for this. She was messy, she smelled of cigarettes and she had asked for the best bedroom in the house, outside of the master, and had gotten it because Mother wanted to avoid a disagreement. Jake and I were in a different part of the house, closer to Mother and Father. Helen had even been able to decorate her room the way she wanted and still she refused to stay in it.

Crawling over my sandal is a spider that I think could be a scorpion even though I have never seen one before. Helen would know for sure but she is asleep. I lie very still until it disappears into the gap between the cement floor and the cinderblock. All night I wait for it to return.

Shortly after Father had gone into Helen's room she moved upstairs. We heard him screaming about the car, the scratch, and the bike. She had leaned her bike against his new grey Cadillac and when it fell by accident it left a dent.

Jake ran downstairs to watch. He told me that when Father started to leave the room, Helen threw *The Grapes of Wrath* in hardback at him. Father, according to Jake, had decided to turn back, probably to say one more thing, at the very same moment that she lobbed the book at his head, but she couldn't have known that the corner would cut him just below his eye, that this was a place that bled profusely. Father lost his breath and when he regained it, he went toward her and grabbed her by her shoulders and shook her before he pushed her against the wall. Specks of his blood stuck to the pale green paint. They were there for years. The maid never noticed and never washed the walls.

Mother did not leave her room. I, too, stayed put.

The next day Helen piled her clothes on the shelves in my closet and cleared three dresser drawers without asking if I minded. This was when she was dating a boy who was a year younger than she was, who seemed thoughtful and gentle. It was unclear to me how he could like her. I wanted him to like me instead.

When Helen settled on a ground floor apartment I left Mexico. For company she bought a puppy that was soon stolen from her front yard. She posted signs offering a reward. The dog snatcher called with the terms. She could pay a sum of money and leave it in a bright red gym bag at the end of the road where new housing was being constructed, or she could do nothing and the dog would be killed. As proof that the dog was dead, he said he would hang her from the electrical wires in front of Helen's house. The road he described was so new it had not yet been named but Helen knew which one. Maybe she hesitated or tried to bargain, but she put the money, in dollars, in a gym bag. Marisol was at her door the next morning. At least it looked like Marisol, but Helen was never completely convinced it was the same dog.

Her apartment is in a gated community but when the guards are held at gunpoint, which happens a few times a year, they let the hooded men inside and don't remember anything about them, what they drove or what they took.

Now Helen owns a beauty salon in a mall downtown and sends me pictures of events: *quinceañeras* parties, weddings and local fashion shows. The *quinceañeras* wear long gowns, some with trains. Helen likes to dress as they do and has the salon photographer take pictures of her, which she binds in an album that sits on the magazine table in the salon. She has everyone guess her age.

For the wedding photographs her hairdresser uses forty-one white flowers, attached to the back of her head with bobby pins and hair glue. I have a photograph of her with flowing hair, extensions from someone else, harvested and ironed onto her thin brittle ends. She sends dozens of images like this. I save them in a file on my computer but I have not thought of a suitable label. "Helen" could work. But I can't say for sure if the photographs really are Helen.

◀ ◀ ◀

Helen is sure. Mother bathed her in the upstairs tub with the yellow washcloth and dried her in the matching towel. Then she rocked on her chair listening to the same song over and over on her forest green record player. It was in French and it began with and repeated many times the name "Dominique ..." When the singing nun's voice stopped, the needle skipped on the flat part of the vinyl until Helen got up and set the arm back at the beginning. She did this many times every night until Father came home. She remembers her polyester, quilted pink robe with the five pink plastic buttons; how she straightened it over her knees, tucking herself inside as if she were a caterpillar in a cocoon.

I wasn't yet born when she waited for him, but I was there when she sat on his lap after dinner, when she stroked his hand, when she got into bed with him on Sunday, when she looked into his eyes and encouraged him to buy something or do something Mother had clearly been against, when she let him rub her back or reach under her shirt to straighten her bra strap, when she rested her head in the crook of his neck and sighed.

◀ ◀ ◀

I don't tell the Photographer no.

It's the end of the day when he parks his van in front of the only restaurant on campus. Had anyone seen us they would have thought I was giving my father a tour. But this father isn't interested in the campus or the curriculum, and Father never visited, even though both of his daughters were matriculated.

The Photographer wants to see my work hanging in the college gallery. The other students' photographs are of corncobs, meadows at sunset, barns and silos. In my series I am dressed in a corduroy jumper and a man-tailored shirt. My white knee socks are trimmed in lace and in each new frame I have removed one more piece of clothing until I am standing naked. It isn't clear what I am holding, not until the last shot, and this is when I offer a red, perfectly formed apple to a nonexistent Adam. The Photographer tells me the photographs of Eve and the apple are genius.

He takes me to a Motel 6 a few miles out on the highway where he unpacks dresses in different shades of magenta. Flapper dresses with low waists and sleeveless ones with a line of tiny fake pearls stitched across the collar. Necklines that plunge so low there is no cover, one that ties, and one with a belt that is soiled and stained. A tube-like dress with pronounced darts under the arms. Something similar to a bathrobe but see-through. Each one smells of mothballs, must, and body odor.

The dogs are with him and pant in the overheated room. In his bag are two flasks; one is vodka, the other bourbon. I can't do this if I am not drunk. He has me try on each dress then photographs me from the corner of the bed.

I wake up on the floor but don't know how long I have been asleep. I don't remember what happened after he got up to change the film, or what time it was. Now, when I lift my head, it's five minutes after three. Outside it is silent, not a car or a truck passes on the interstate.

His clothes are off and he is asleep between the dresses.

I hear the heavy breathing of the other men who have been in this motel room, their women pinned beneath them, who, like me, wanted to run but didn't. I get up.

I open the motel door slowly, after making sure I didn't leave anything. I do not stop running until I reach the evenly plowed furrows on the opposite side of the highway. The ground has little mirrors of frost patterned across a tractor's tread. I wrap myself in my coat and nuzzle my cheek into the collar. Using cornhusks for a pillow I wait. By sunrise the birds have settled on the stalks and there are fresh piles of shit.

I estimate the Photographer is well on his way when I begin to walk back to school. In the common room in the dormitory where I live the television set is on. I don't recognize the girl watching and she is so high she doesn't realize I am in the room even after the couch makes a squeaking noise as I sit.

He didn't have an eye for architecture or nature, only girls, girls in rodeos, in museums, at yard sales, in classrooms, behind desks like the ones in the classrooms where he taught, girls in restaurants who served, the grocery store cashier girl, the girl who could do Hula-Hoops on the front lawn for hours at a time and the skipping-rope girls. It isn't possible to be with him and go for very long without seeing him watching his girls.

Had I not agreed I would have, at the very least—I should have—brought it to the attention of an adult. Then I might feel as if I did one thing right.

◀ ◀ ◀

If I can fall asleep, which most nights I can't, I wake after an hour and it isn't until the sun is rising that I begin to dream.

Mother kept different strengths of Valium on the middle shelf of her medicine chest. I took a few every month when she first filled the prescription. That way there always seemed to be enough for us both.

The appointment with the college shrink is brief. At the time I didn't understand her questioning but now I see where she was going. She says something about a father. The father. Father. I start sobbing in quaking heaves and when I catch my breath all I am able to do is ask for a prescription. She counts out five tablets and slides them into a tiny manila envelope. A refill requires a return visit.

I collect my books and coat.

She thrusts the box of tissues in front of me.

I push her hand away. The tissues are pink and scented like the ones Grandmother once offered.

◀ ◀ ◀

My roommate and I would get high and walk through the woods behind the concrete dorms. She wore a long dress of course muslin with flowers stenciled at the border. I remember her finding a wad of money on the trail. She tucked it into her pocket, telling me we would divide it later. She never gave me my half. I don't know if she kept it for herself, or maybe we never found any money at all.

In the same woods we took off our clothes and hung them from a branch and buried ourselves under pine needles. She lost a shoe. We missed dinner.

When the summer session ended, Helen and her friend picked me up. I took pictures of them. Her friend looks like the man in the Grant Wood painting with a pitchfork and overalls. Helen wears a peasant blouse and the space between her teeth makes her look young, even younger than me.

After having been home a week, I visit my roommate at her parents' house in Connecticut while her family is vacationing on the Cape. She keeps the house dark, not opening the blinds or turning on the lights. It is sometime after nine when she lights candles. She asked me to bring drugs but I didn't and she is angry with me. If she wasn't so distressed I would like the way she looks, pouting from a reclining position on a heavily pillowed couch reading Emma Goldman.

I bring her raw cookie batter, and when I put the remainder in the oven she draws a bath in her parents' tub, adding juniper salts. I sit on the side of the tub while she floats. Her hair covers half her face. We smoke a joint. I remove my clothes and slide into the tub. The cookies burn.

I try to get into her bed but she points across the room and says, the guest bed is yours. I wander through the house looking at her parents' possessions. Batiks from Bali, tiny china sets from

Tibet, metal sculptures of geometric shapes, and shallow dishes of potpourri.

The next morning before she wakes up I walk to the train station.

I want to bury the photographs I took in her parents' house of stuffed snakes hanging from her bedpost, the shag rug beneath her feet, a girl alone in a tub of bubbles. Instead I move them to the top shelf of my closet thinking if it is difficult for me to get to them I will eventually stop needing to see her. Still, several times a day I stand on the desk chair and pull each photograph down and hold it in my hands. One photograph is of a million pine needles. In it, she is washing the sap from my feet.

◀ ◀ ◀

In Havana I take photographs of the sea wall. Metal mesh protrudes from the concrete benches, leaving a pattern of rust. An old man looks out. The angles of the bench and the pier jutting into the water position him in the center of a maze.

The Photographer and I swim in the sea outside our hotel, a run-down skyscraper of faded chintz and tattered carpets that could have been a haven for drug dealers, gamblers, and their prostitutes. There is a much older man on our tour, who says he is a communist, a Jew from New York City. He thinks we have this in common, this Jewishness. The Photographer and I swim while he watches us from the shore.

Carlos and Rosita are in the room next to us. They left as children and had somehow been able to secure passage back with our group. Rosita fills her pocketbook with leftover food. I heard her say she has money sewn into the seams of her skirts and the cuffs of Carlos's pants. When they can, they leave the group to visit relatives. Each day she wears a different color of plastic hoops. Three weeks later when we leave, Rosita is not wearing earrings. I do not know for sure but I think the outfits she wore also disappeared. What I notice is how easy it is for her to lift her suitcase onto the bus on our last day.

The one in our group I want to see me is Nathan. Not the old communist Jew or the Photographer. I imagine Nathan was once a guerilla, that he knew Che. He is thin and fragile and walks with a slight limp. His Spanish is beautiful, from Uruguay, so different from the quickly swallowed words of Carlos and Rosita. At the end of the trip all of us exchange phone numbers. Months later, I try just one time to call Nathan. The number he wrote down on our last day, only after I asked him for it more than once, is a non-working number.

The old communist Jew is waiting for us when we get out of the water. He comes in close and touches my left breast.

Instinctively I jump away.

The Photographer says to me, take it easy.

I glare at him.

The old communist Jew says, I was removing this, and holds up a piece of seaweed he has pulled out of my bathing suit top.

The Photographer laughs.

All of us go to the Tropicana nightclub. The women are still here, twenty years after Batista, dancing on tables for men. We drink rum and tonic and pay in dollars. I have their photographs. Their boas and costumes are restitched in different-colored threads. They now look more like clowns than seductresses. There is something wild in one of the dancer's eyes, while the others look worn and tired. These photographs are on a separate roll of film from the ones I took earlier in the day.

The Photographer had stayed at the hotel, preferring the sun. I wandered along the road that led down to the sea. Children smiled for me. One played with a stick whittled in the shape of a gun. While walking back to where we were staying an army officer stopped me and confiscated the roll of film I had just shot, but he did not take my camera. He asked if I had more exposed film, and when I told him no, he didn't go through my pockets or my knapsack.

Back home in my darkroom in my parents' house I develop roll after roll and one, to my surprise, is from that afternoon. The officer must have slipped it back into my bag after I was in his jeep. He said he needed to take me to my hotel and knew where I was staying without asking.

Musicians play for us each night and in the mornings the bus takes us to hospitals, farms, day care centers, passing the Bacardi mansion in the center of town. Its shutters have been splintered by gale winds. Out front, men play dominoes. I have close-up shots of the ivory tiles, handled so many times the white surface is smooth and concave. One man lets me hold the one with seven dots. Never before had I touched real ivory.

All my photographs are better than the ones the Photographer shot, and when he looks through them he says, I wasn't feeling well that trip.

◀ ◀ ◀

I am accustomed to the Photographer. He doesn't keep me waiting and every Wednesday there is a letter from him in my mailbox. He hasn't forgotten a birthday and once a week he calls. But this time when he tells me he plans to visit, I tell him, no, something I have never done before.

I drop the receiver and let it dangle and stare at it as it sways back and forth like a metronome, occasionally tapping the sides of the booth. The girl who looks like a replica of Marilyn Monroe walks by, waiving the keys to her white convertible Cadillac. She stops to hang up the phone and when it rings, almost immediately, I tell her, you haven't seen me, make something up about my disappearance or death.

Marilyn Monroe says, one moment please, and cups her hand over the receiver. She waits a minute to make it seem as if she is looking for me, before bringing the phone to her red lipsticked lips: There is a note on the chalkboard on her door that says, I am leaving school. Don't look for me."

His voice is loud enough for the other girl in front of the television to hear but she isn't listening. He says, I was on the phone with her two minutes ago. She couldn't have gone far. Look in the bathroom, call out her name. See if you can catch her.

You were the last person she spoke to? Marilyn purses her lips. How did she sound?

He's screaming at Marilyn Monroe, not knowing it is Marilyn Monroe. You're wasting time, go check. It's urgent.

I am sorry but it's not my job to hunt her down. Here in this dorm we all answer the phone and knock on the door of the person the caller is looking for, and when the person is not there we are simply required to leave a message. Would you like to do that?

Do what?

Leave a message.

You need to look for her.

No sir, I need not do anything further so I will ask you one last time, do you want to leave a message?

Why can't you just call her name in the hallway?

It's probably a joke. I really have to go. Marilyn Monroe positions the phone in its cradle one last time.

We are laughing. She prances towards her room and turns toward me, let me know how it turns out.

Can I ask a favor? Will you let me photograph you as Marilyn?
Of course.
In full makeup and hairdo?
The whole thing.

I have her spread her legs over a sewer grate. Her white chiffon skirt catches the wind and circles around her. She uses her hands to pat down the sides of her skirt so it doesn't fly over her head. But the coquettish expression in the original photograph makes no sense. I have my Marilyn wrap her face in gauze. It prints out white and featureless.

◀ ◀ ◀

Instead of dogs this man has a girlfriend. His name is the same as the Photographer's and her name is mine. We look similar. Our hair color, the shape of our eyes, our build. She pours shots of tequila as he undoes the buttons of her shirt. I watch, not knowing what else to do.

She pushes him to the side and takes my arm and helps me undress, folding my shirt and pants, using her hand as an iron to make a perfect crease. She collects my bra and underwear from the floor. He is pinning me under him.

I look her in the eye. She watches.

When he is done with me, he crushes her neck between his hands and her white winter skin goes ruddy red. I am afraid she isn't breathing. He releases his grip and she coughs for a long time. It takes a few more minutes before I am convinced she is okay.

When the three of us are finished, she is the first to get up from his bed, holding the sheet in front of her.

What we just did—they have done before, this very same way, the two of them leading a third.

We reach for our clothing and inside out our pant legs and shirtsleeves.

I need help, she says.

I don't know what she means.

The meal, she continues while trying to tie the belt of her terry cloth bathrobe.

He must know what's next. He is fastening his belt and I am buttoning my shirt before reaching for my sneakers.

Cucumber and yogurt soup, she says.

From across the room she hands me the sharpest knife. I follow her into the small kitchen that is shared by three adjoining suites.

She has found fresh dill in the middle of the winter. I do not tell her I dislike dill, that it is too sweet, that it reminds me of

Father who mixes it with sour cream and slathers it on cold salmon to kill the flavor of fish.

The yogurt won't drop from the spoon into the metal measuring cup. She has a desperate look. When it does land, an air bubble in the center concerns her and she waits for it to settle. When it doesn't, she begins to bang the container on its side. It is as if she must calibrate the amount precisely or else there will be consequences. I am afraid for her. She is too tired to care this much about details.

She slices cucumber, thin like tracing paper. The seeds make a pattern in threes. Greenish marks rise below her ear where it merges with her neck. I want to run my fingers over my throat to see if this bruising is also happening to me. Beginning with my collarbone I feel for swelling. My neck aches from straining into the contorted angles I assumed, as I tried to please them, him especially.

At the small table our six knees knock. I push my chair back so I am no longer a part of their circle. We didn't speak at dinner in our house. Mother attended to Father, anticipating his next need, and if there was a problem with my sister that day they avoided discussing it until dinner was over.

Do you like the soup?

He nods.

More?

I shake my head no, then pick up my dish and begin washing. It's the right thing to do. She did the shopping, the cooking, and all of the planning.

Although he has eaten everything, he does not help clean up. When the kitchen is in order, I thank her. She gets up and comes towards me, wanting to embrace. He watches from his seat at the table. I step away.

The cold air stings my face, especially where his unshaven stubble scraped my cheek and neck. I walk home, not noticing anyone or the color of the light. I am unsteady—maybe a pulled muscle or from exhaustion. Before I shower, I write to the Photographer.

Dear Richard,
Found another Richard.
No dogs but another woman. Also a Leslie. There is that photograph of twin girls by Diane Arbus. The curls in their hair are the same, their features, too. One could leave and an identical one would be left.
Leslie.

I put the letter in an envelope and stamp it. Before I go into the bathroom I search my desk drawer. I find the photograph the Photographer took of me when I was fifteen. It is the only photograph of his that I have. He doesn't know I took it that day he was too drunk to drive me home. I put it in the envelope behind the letter and seal it.

Is it the neck of the goose prepared for slaughter, or the skin of the wild bird after the feathers have been plucked, gooseflesh? As I get into the tub the water is not deep enough to cover even my legs. I am so cold I should have waited for the bath to be drawn before getting in. The blood from my torn membranes turns the bubbles in the water pink. I close my eyes hoping the tub will fill and that as it does the water will lose its tint. There is such poor pressure I am afraid there will never be enough water, that I will freeze waiting. I pull my towel over my shoulders and bury my face in it. Not waiting any longer, I get out, dragging the towel along the floor, walking with difficulty—my inner thighs ache—like when I was young and Father took me and Helen to ride horses.
I load film into my camera and photograph the white linoleum floor where my blood has already hardened.
I decide to leave it there.
For the rest of the year, every time I use that bathroom, I see

my blood. Not until I pack at the end of school do I scrub the stain. A bloodstain is hard to clean. There is some property of blood that resists water.

Pink bubbles cling to my heel, refusing to disappear. It is the same pink I see every year when I blow out the candles on my birthday cake, even though there is no pink taste. The green buttercream leaves are the color of the cucumber she served and the color of bruised skin that formed on her neck. The lettering reads Happy Birthday in gel frosting, the color of his eyes.

◀ ◀ ◀

I drop out of the college in the cornfield and buy a plane ticket to Belfast. The first series I shoot is from the back of a bus. I reach my hands holding the camera through the jagged edges of shattered glass.

On the border between the two sides of the city I see a small girl, alone. I signal to the bus driver this is my stop. The girl is wearing a plaid skirt and her shirt is buttoned incorrectly. The playground is of chains hanging. There is no adult to ask if I can take her picture, and when I suggest it, she smiles. Her feet bend inward, her hands jut out from her sides like loosely hanging branches needing support and water. Her hair is dark and her skin fair and freckled. It doesn't look as if it has been brushed in a long time. The skirt and shirt she is wearing are part of the school uniform, a traditional navy and green plaid. Her socks are scrunched around her ankles, the elastic no longer doing its job.

She asks if I want to watch her swing. We walk away from the metal gate that encloses the playground. Sparse sprigs of grass press against the asphalt, as do weeds, some with tiny colored flowers. On the swing she pumps her legs, bending her knees and when she flies out of the range of the viewfinder, the camera misses her. But I see her as she nearly rounds the metal bar at the top of the swing set.

Only I am afraid.

I am given the name of a family on the outskirts of town that runs a bed and breakfast. Their home is in a field of peat. I walk for a long time from the village center through the countryside to reach it. There are no other guests. The man is a volunteer firefighter and his wife warns me that during the night the alarm might sound. Above my bed are two things, a red bell that does go off in the night, and a picture of Jesus that looks like a paint-by-number drawing.

There is one tub, the one she and her husband use. They have no children. I ask permission to bathe because I need her to turn the boiler on and I need a towel.

She brings me a hand towel and the skeleton key. I am afraid the coil heater might electrocute me and decide against running a bath.

After breakfast I pay the woman. Her husband is already gone. I want to turn back and ask if she's afraid of the hot water heater, about her life in the middle of nowhere with a man who fights fires, and about the Jesus Christ—had she painted it, and why she hesitated when all I did was ask for a towel. Instead, I photograph the lupine and foxglove, and when I'm done, I turn back and look towards the house one last time. She is watching from an open window. She waves. Not a goodbye, more of an acknowledgment. Her eyes, like the eyes of the girl on the swing, are full of things I do not know.

Along the road I come across an old woman holding a cat. I have her picture. Her skin is mottled and patchy like the destroyed mortar of the brick apartments surrounding her.

I am searched before the policeman allows me to enter the outdoor market. Women hurry from fish vendor to fruit seller without speaking.

◀ ◀ ◀

I stored years of photographs in black-bottomed 8x10 boxes with shiny orange tops. I preferred a paper called Portriga that has a brownish hue. It made my photographs appear as if they had been preserved from some other time. Sepia, I hoped, would disguise them.

I also used a paper called Brovira, which produces a colder image. Brovira's blacks are very black and the whites pure. Overall, it was too stark a choice for most of my images. Photographic paper was expensive and I never discarded anything, not even the mistakes. I wrote on the box tops the range of dates for the photographs inside, and if the place was important I would write that as well. I rarely looked at these prints because I mounted the perfected images onto matte board to preserve them before storing each one in the large red portfolio. Eventually floods and mice and neglect ate through the red weld but most of the mounted prints survived, even though many are spotted with mold.

I stored my negatives in a loose-leaf binder after I carefully slid them into glycine envelopes. I always took them with me to all the places I lived, even though I never referred back to them. When I left college for the summer, I kicked a cardboard moving box containing all theses things into the common room, to be picked up by maintenance and stored. I did not label them with enough information and for many months they were lost. I argued with the school to try to find them even though I knew it had been my fault. It wasn't the first time I had tried to lose them. Eventually they showed up and I carried them with me for many years thereafter. Each time I left the country, I put them in storage.

On another occasion I left behind my negatives as well as my camera. I should have seen this as a warning, the leaving of the camera. I had never been without it, not at any other time. Again I spent months trying to get these things back. And again I eventually found someone to send them to me.

Why, at each turn, did I make myself prove—by having to put forth such hard work just to win back what was mine—that they not only belonged to me, but that I had made them? When this last batch was returned I had many of the negatives reprinted just in case. But I hadn't printed them and they weren't the same. They were only half mine.

Finally, and it had to be, all the boxes with the orange tops and black bottoms were thrown away. I left it up to the person moving into my apartment, who clearly would not have known what was valuable or not, to sort through my things and discard whatever seemed unnecessary. The water-stained prints, the reams of negatives, the heavy boxes of years and years of work, all of them, she determined had no value.

◀ ◀ ◀

Recently, I took photographs of my body. Raised rivers of veins, wrinkled flesh, inexplicable indentations, the scarring and sinuous ridges from the surgeons' scalpels. No one will see these images. I did not wash the paper properly. In time the chemicals will turn them an eerie purple and the image will disappear. There is some property to the silver in the paper that makes the image unstable. It may be similar to what gives an old mirror its mirrorness, which in time degrades, and as it does a lace burnished in black creeps through the glass. Like the negative or print that has begun to disintegrate, in time the mirror no longer reflects an image, only the memory of one.

Seeing no need to continue I put my camera into storage.

◀ ◀ ◀

I am outside my apartment locking the door when the elevator opens. The Photographer looks left then right and when he sees me, he picks up his gait. Leaning into my door he lets me know he wants to go inside, to find something of me, a telling object, maybe nothing more than a lost eyelash still floating in the morning's coffee cup, and capture it to take it with him when he leaves, to catalogue it with his possessions of me that need updating.

I will not allow him to take one more thing.

Do you have dogs? I want to see your dogs.

No, no dogs.

We hear them panting on the other side of the door.

We study each other. For me, I need to see him for verification that it happened. Some sort of proof.

He leans towards me to touch my hair. I pull back.

We walk down the hallway.

He doesn't seem any older. Is now then, or is it that then will never be in the past, that when it concerns the Photographer, there is no past?

By having done nothing all these years I didn't protect the others that must have come after me.

I sit across from him in a diner.

He speaks about nothing as if he can turn nothing into something. It's how he always spoke, I was just too young to know.

I loved you, really loved you. He says. I thought I was dying.

We all think we are dying. It's the last thing I say to him.

Before I went into the hospital I burned all the images of you, even the negatives, to protect you.

Protect you, is what I keep hearing as I lose all sensation. I look at my legs and don't recognize their shape or size. My hands do not feel connected to my arms. I lift the left one and like a puppeteer direct it toward my face. I clear my throat. All I am thinking about is how to move my legs and when I have gone over the procedure a number of times I begin by sliding across the seat. When I reach the end of the bench, I take my sweater and my bag. He is still talking but I can't focus on his words, they no longer make sense.

He trails behind me, having stayed to pay the check.

I think I hear him ask, Can we do this again?

Walking in front of me is a father. The father holds his daughter's little pink hand that has a tiny gold ring on her pointer finger. The ring has a red stone in the shape of a heart. They are talking about horseback riding in Central Park. The little girl drops a pink sweater with yellow flowers and pale pink buttons. I pick it up and run a few steps. When I catch up to them, I hope they might let me walk alongside them for a block, just one, but the father takes the sweater and thanks me and walks faster.

I trail behind the little girl wearing my sweater, or is it Helen's, and the father who is nothing like Father.

◀ ◀ ◀

That night I dream the Photographer is spying on me. I am at my desk and he is standing behind a partition. Something rustles. It takes me a few frozen moments to gather the courage to look. And when I do I see him standing in the shadows.

This dream keeps waking me. Then for no reason it stops.

The next time it comes, I dream I am in bed with my husband and the Photographer is watching me through a crack in the wall that I had never noticed. I do not see the Photographer's whole body, just his eyes and the bridge of his nose and the frame of his glasses.

New dreams keep coming.

I am walking across the street after having left my apartment building and he is on the front stoop of a building on the far left.

I am in front of the kitchen sink washing an apple and he is in the apartment across the way staring through a telescope.

I am walking the dog in the park and he is on the stone wall overlooking the West Side Highway, staring down at me. He is the size of a monument. The dog begins to pull on his leash, and when I do not move, because I am afraid, he begins to whimper.

I try drinking cognac to get back to sleep. I take warm baths. I boil milk. I watch the cars outside the front window of my apartment and concentrate on the sounds they make. I read picture books from my childhood and from my children's childhood.

I am given medicine to make me sleep.

I still take this medicine.

◀ ◀ ◀

Jake lives in Mother and Father's basement. He has filled it with guitars. Once he had no more than three, but now there are so many I can only estimate, maybe thirty-five?

They lean against the couch, are stashed in the corners of the room, or stacked on top of open cases lined in velvet. Sheet music is piled next to Mother's metronome, packages of strings made of nylon and steel, some half-open, hang. Tiny bottles of oil in different-colored hues, the scratch-free polishing rags.

Jake has a pile of tuners, all in the same shape as the flying saucers we lined up to buy in summer. He ate the ones with vanilla middles and could eat as many as five. Helen and I preferred the ones filled with chocolate.

He keeps electric guitars, some neon in wild-shaped triangles. There are straps made of silk, in leather and with tiny plastic beads. Faux tortoiseshell picks and in every other color, some chewed, some dulled from use, others still shiny and new.

When he walks upstairs Jake is a child again.

I see Father in his wheelchair in the foyer, slumped over asleep and imagine that there are nights Mother just parks him there until morning, not bothering to put him into bed. I wonder if Jake has noticed.

◀ ◀ ◀

I see Father a week before he dies. He doesn't look like Father. There is nothing powerful about him. His arms and hands that were once muscular, that ripped the deer's front and hind legs, that touched my sister, are now shriveled.

He knows who I am most of the time. Just once he calls me Helen. When I ask how he spends his days, he tells me he watches the woods.

What do you watch in the woods?

Deer. I'm always looking for deer. They are hungry, even starving.

Don't they eat?

He is confused by the question, but eventually says, each deer is distinct. I remember one I have seen if I see it again.

He takes out a grocery receipt and a pencil from his shirt pocket.

What is that, Daddy?

I called him Daddy.

A tally card.

What are you keeping tally of? He looks at me as if I am no longer speaking a language he recognizes. You were telling me you look for deer, is that what you keep a list of?

Yes, of how many but also which ones. I have a code based on appearances, two spots, dark amber, and so on, and if it is a fawn I make a mark like this. He shows me the card. And for a doe or a buck, I note it this way. He takes a pencil and draws a **D** and then a **B**.

I nod but I don't understand. The marks aren't consistent and don't seem to go across the page left to right, and some run into the mark before it or following it.

Your mother thinks I'm making it up but it isn't something I would make up.

Why are you keeping this list?

They have poisoned the deer. There won't be another generation. Don't you follow the news? He is annoyed with me.

They give the deer something that makes them sterile.

He knows the details of the town's plan. He understands it completely, almost down to the wording of the ordinance.

It isn't a good idea to poison the next generation.

Can I get you anything?

Rusty.

What did you say?

Rusty.

Nothing is rusted in the house. Mother takes good care of everything.

My dog Rusty.

He remembers the dog that Grandmother told us he strangled.

I didn't kill that dog. I loved him.

Then he starts to cry like a child. The way I cried when I was little and got hurt, in deep heaves where it is difficult to stop and catch your breath.

Dad, it's okay, don't worry about Rusty. Not anymore.

I didn't mean to do it.

You didn't?

I promise Helen, I didn't.

He called me Helen. It scares me and I have to get up and leave the room. I go to the corner of the porch and look out to the woods. When I go back to where he is seated the pencil is poised in his hand. I wonder if he thinks I am a deer. If he has tallied me in as a doe.

Books from Etruscan Press

Etruscan Press Is Proud of Support Received From

Wilkes University

Youngstown State University

The Raymond John Wean Foundation

The Ohio Arts Council

The Stephen & Jeryl Oristaglio Foundation

The Nathalie & James Andrews Foundation

The National Endowment for the Arts

The Ruth H. Beecher Foundation

The Bates-Manzano Fund

The New Mexico Community Foundation

Drs. Barbara Brothers & Gratia Murphy Fund

Ohio Arts Council
A STATE AGENCY
THAT SUPPORTS PUBLIC
PROGRAMS IN THE ARTS

NATIONAL
ENDOWMENT
FOR THE ARTS
A great nation
deserves great art.

Founded in 2001 with a generous grant from the Oristaglio Foundation, Etruscan Press is a nonprofit cooperative of poets and writers working to produce and promote books that nurture the dialogue among genres, achieve a distinctive voice, and reshape the literary and cultural histories of which we are a part.

etruscan press
www.etruscanpress.org

Etruscan Press books may be ordered from

Consortium Book Sales and Distribution
800.283.3572
www.cbsd.com

Small Press Distribution
800.869.7553
www.spdbooks.org